The
CREATURE
in the CASE

An Old Kingdom story, set approximately six
months after the events in *Abhorsen*.

The
CREATURE
in the CASE

GARTH
NIX

HarperCollins *Children's Books*

First published for World Book Day in Great Britain by
Harper Collins *Children's Books* 2005
Harper Collins *Children's Books* is a division of HarperCollins *Publishers* Ltd
77-85 Fulham Palace Road, Hammersmith, London, W6 8JB

www.harpercollinschildrensbooks.co.uk

1 3 5 7 9 8 6 4 2

Copyright © Garth Nix 2005

ISBN 0 00 720138 9

Garth Nix asserts the moral right to be
identified as the author of the work.

Printed and bound in Great Britain by
Bookmarque Ltd, Croydon, Surrey

"I am going back to the Old Kingdom, Uncle," said Nicholas Sayre. "Whatever father may have told you. So there is no point you trying to fix me up with a suitable Sayre job or a suitable Sayre marriage. I am coming with you to what will undoubtedly be a horrendous house party only because it will get me a few hundred miles closer to the Wall."

Nicholas's Uncle Edward, more generally known as The Most Honourable Edward Sayre, Chief Minister of Ancelstierre, shut the red-bound letter book he was reading with more emphasis than he intended, as their heavily-armoured car lurched over a hump in the road. The sudden clap of the book made the bodyguard in front look round, but their driver kept his eyes on the narrow country lane.

"Have I said anything about a job or a marriage?" Edward enquired, gazing down his long patrician nose at his nineteen-year-old nephew. "Besides, you won't even get within a mile of the Perimeter without a pass signed by me, let alone across the Wall."

"I could get a pass from Lewis," said Nicholas moodily, referring to the newly-anointed Hereditary Arbiter. The previous Arbiter, Lewis's grandfather, had died of a heart attack during Corolini's attempted coup d'etat half a year before.

"No you couldn't, and you know it," said Edward. "Lewis has more sense than to involve himself in any aspect of government other than the ceremonial."

"Then I'll have to cross over without a pass," declared Nicholas angrily, not even trying to hide the anger and frustration that had built up in him over the past six months that he'd been forced to stay in Ancelstierre. Most of that time spent wishing he'd left with Lirael and Sam in the immediate aftermath of the Destroyer's defeat, instead of deciding he should try and recuperate in Ancelstierre. Weakness and fear had driven that decision, combined with a desire to put the terrible past behind him. But he now knew that was impossible. He could not ignore the legacy of his involvement with Hedge and the Destroyer, nor his return to Life at the hands – or the paws – of the Disreputable Dog. He had become someone else, and he could only find out who that was in the Old Kingdom.

"You would almost certainly be shot if you try to cross illegally," said Edward. "Which you would richly deserve. Particularly since you are not giving me the opportunity to help you. I do not know why you or anyone else would want to go to the Old Kingdom – my year on the

Perimeter as General Hort's ADC certainly taught me that the place is best avoided. Nor do I wish to annoy your father and hurt your mother, but there *are* certain circumstances in which I might grant you permission to cross the Perimeter."

"What! Really?"

"Yes, really. Have I ever taken you or any other of my nephews or nieces to a house party before?"

"Not that I know—"

"Do I usually make a habit of attending parties given by someone like Alastor Dorrance in the middle of nowhere?"

"I suppose not..."

"Then you might exercise your intelligence to wonder why you are here with me now."

"Gatehouse ahead, sir," interrupted the bodyguard as the car rounded a sweeping corner and slowed down. "Recognition signal is correct."

Both Edward and Nicholas leaned forward to look through the open partition and the windscreen beyond. A few hundred yards ahead, a squat stone gatehouse lurked just off the road, with its two wooden gates swung back. Two slate-grey Heddon-Hare roadsters were parked either side of the gate, with several mackintosh-clad, weapon-toting men standing around them. One of the men waved a yellow flag in a series of complicated movements, that Edward clearly understood and Nicholas presumed meant all was well.

"Proceed!" snapped the Chief Minister. Their car slowed more, the driver shifting down through the gears with practised double declutching. The mackintosh-clad men saluted as the car swung off the road and through the gate, dropping their salute as the rest of the motorcade followed. Six motorcycle policemen were immediately behind, then another two cars identical to the one that carried Nicholas and his uncle, then another half dozen police motorcyclists and finally four trucks that were carrying a company of fully-armed soldiery. Corolini's attempted putsch had failed and there had surprisingly been no further trouble from the "Our Country" party since, but the government continued to be nervous about the safety of the nation's chief minister.

"So what is going on?" asked Nicholas. "Why are you here? And why am I here? Is there is something you want me to do?"

"At last, a glimmer of thought. Have you ever wondered what Alastor Dorrance actually does, other than come to Corvere three or four times a year and exercise his eccentricities in public?"

"Isn't that enough?" asked Nick with a shudder. He remembered the newspaper stories from the last time Dorrance had been in the city, only a few weeks before. He'd hosted a picnic on Holyoak Hill for every apprentice in Corvere and supplied them with fatty roast beef, copious amounts of beer, and a particularly cheap and nasty red wine, with predictable results.

"Dorrance's eccentricities are all show," said Edward. "Misdirection. He is in fact the head of Department Thirteen. Dorrance Hall is the department's main research facility."

"But Department Thirteen is just a made-up thing, for the moving pictures. It doesn't really exist... um... does it?"

"Officially, no. In actuality, yes. Every state has need of spies. Department Thirteen trains and manages ours, and carries out various tasks ill-suited to more regular arms of government. It is watched over quite carefully, I assure you."

"But what has that got to do with me?"

"Department Thirteen observes all our neighbours very successfully, and has detailed files on everyone and everything important within those countries. With one notable exception. The Old Kingdom."

"I'm not going to spy on my friends!"

Edward sighed and looked out of the window. The drive beyond the gatehouse curved through freshly-mown fields, the hay already gathered into small hillocks ready to be pitchforked into carts and taken to the stacks. Past the fields, he could make out the chimneys of a large country house peering above the fringe of old oaks that lined the drive.

"I'm not going to be a spy, Uncle," repeated Nicholas.

"I haven't asked you to be one," said Edward as he looked back at his nephew. Nicholas's face had paled and he was clutching his chest. Whatever had happened to him

9

in the Old Kingdom had left him in a very run-down state and he was still recovering. The Ancelstierran doctors had found no external sign of significant injury, and his X-rays came out strangely fogged, but all the medical reports said Nick was in the same sort of shape as a man who had suffered serious wounds in battle.

"All I want you to do is to spend the weekend here with some of the Department's technical people," continued Edward. "Answer their questions about your experiences in the Old Kingdom, that sort of thing. I doubt that anything will come of it, and as you know, I strictly adhere to the wisdom of my predecessors, which is to leave the place alone. But that said, they haven't exactly left us alone over the past twenty years. Dorrance has always had a bit of a bee in his bonnet about the Old Kingdom, greatly exacerbated by the... mmm... event at Forwin Mill. It is possible that he might discover something useful from talking to you. So if you answer his questions, you shall have your Perimeter pass on Monday morning. If you're still set on going, that is."

"I'll cross the Wall," said Nick forcefully. "One way or another."

"Then I suggest it be my way. You know, your father wanted to be a painter when he was your age. He had talent too, according to old Menree. But our parents wouldn't hear of it. A grave error, I think. Not that he hasn't been a useful politician, and a great help to me. But his heart is elsewhere, and it is not possible to achieve greatness without a whole heart."

"So all I have to do is answer questions?"

Edward sighed the sigh of an older and wiser man talking to a younger, inattentive and impatient relative.

"Well, you will have to appear a little bit at the party. Dinner and so forth. Croquet perhaps, or a row on the lake. Misdirection, as I said."

Nicholas took Edward's hand and shook it firmly.

"You are a splendid uncle, Uncle."

"Good. I'm glad that's settled," said Edward. He glanced out of the window. They were past the oak trees now, gravel crunching beneath the wheels as the car rolled up the drive to the front steps of the six-columned entrance. "We'll drop you off then, and I'll see you Monday."

"Aren't you staying here? For the house party?"

"Don't be silly! I can't abide house parties, of any kind. I'm staying at the Golden Sheaf. Excellent hotel, not too far away. I often go there to get through some serious confidential reading. Place's got its own golf course, too. Thought I might go round tomorrow. Enjoy yourself!"

Nicholas hardly caught the last two words as his door was flung open and he was assisted out by Edward's personal bodyguard. He blinked in the late afternoon sunlight, no longer filtered through the smoked glass of the car windows. A few seconds later, his bags were deposited at his feet, then the Chief Minister's cavalcade started up again and rolled out the drive as quickly as it had arrived, the Army trucks leaving considerable ruts in the gravel.

"Mr Sayre?"

Nicholas looked around. A top-hatted footman was picking up his bags, but it was another man who had spoken. A balding, burly individual in a dark blue suit, his hair cut so short it was practically a monkish tonsure. Everything about him said policeman, either active or recently retired.

"Yes, I'm Nicholas Sayre."

"Welcome to Dorrance Hall, sir. My name is Hedge—"

Nicholas recoiled from the offered hand and nearly fell over the footman. Even as he regained his balance, he realised that the man had said "Hodge" and then followed it up with a second syllable.

"Hodgeman." Not "Hedge."

Hedge the necromancer was finally, completely and utterly dead. Lirael and the Disreputable Dog had defeated him, and Hedge had gone beyond the Ninth Gate. He couldn't come back. Nick knew he was safe from him, but that knowledge was purely intellectual. Deep inside, the name of Hedge was linked irrevocably with an almost primal fear.

"Sorry," gasped Nick. He straightened up and shook the man's hand. "Ankle gave way on me. You were saying?"

"Hodgeman is my name. I am an assistant to Mr Dorrance. The other guests do not arrive till later today, so Mr Dorrance thought you might like a tour of the grounds?"

"Um, certainly," replied Nick. He fought back a sudden urge to look around to see who might be listening, and as he started up the steps, resisted the temptation to slink from shadow to shadow like a spy in a moving picture.

"The house was originally built in the time of the last Trouin-Durville Pretender, about four hundred years ago, but little of the original structure remains. Most of the current house was built by Mr Dorrance's grandfather. The best feature is the library, which was formerly the great hall of the old house. Shall we start there?"

"Thank you," replied Nicholas. Mr Hodgeman's turn as a tour guide was quite convincing. He wondered if the man had to do it often for casual visitors, as part of what Uncle Edward would call 'misdirection'.

The library was very impressive. Hodgeman closed the double doors behind them as Nick stared up at the high dome of the ceiling, which was painted to create the illusion of a storm at sea. It was quite disconcerting to look up at the waves and the tossing ships, and the low-scudding clouds. Below the dome, every wall was covered by shelves, stretching up twenty or even twenty-five feet from the floor. Ladders ran on rails around the library, but no one was using them. The library was silent, the circular lounge in the centre empty. The windows were heavily curtained with velvet drapes, but the gas lanterns above the shelves burnt very brightly. The place looked like there should be people reading in it, or sorting books, or something. It did not have the dark, dusty air of a disused library.

"This way, sir," said Hodgeman. He crossed to one of the shelves and reached up above his head to pull out an unobtrusive, dun-coloured tome, adorned only with the Dorrance coat of arms, a chain *Argent issuant* from a chevron *Argent* upon a field *Azure*.

The book slid out half way, then came no further.

Hodgeman looked up at it. Nick looked too.

"Is something supposed to happen?"

"It gets a bit stuck sometimes," replied Hodgeman. He tugged on the book again. This time it came completely out. Hodgeman opened it, took a key from its hollowed-out pages, pushed two books apart on the shelf below to reveal a keyhole, inserted the key and turned it. There was a soft click, but nothing more dramatic. Hodgeman put the key back in the book and returned the volume to the shelf.

"Now, if you wouldn't mind stepping this way," Hodgeman said, leading Nick back to the centre of the library. The crescent-shaped lounges had moved aside on silent gears, and two steel-encased segments of the floor had slid open, revealing a circular stone staircase leading down. Unlike the library's brilliant white gas lights, the stairwell was lit by dull electric bulbs.

"This is all rather cloak-and-dagger," remarked Nick as he headed down the steps, with Hodgeman close behind him.

Hodgeman didn't answer, but Nick was sure a disapproving glance had fallen on his back. The steps went down quite a long way, at least equivalent to three or four floors. They ended in front of a steel door with a covered spyhole. Hodgeman pressed a tarnished bronze bell-button next to the door and a few seconds later, the spyhole slid open.

"Sergeant Hodgeman with Mr Nicholas Sayre," said Hodgeman.

The door swung open. There was no sign of a person behind it. Just a long, dismal, white-painted concrete corridor stretching off some thirty or forty yards to another steel door. Nick stepped through the doorway and some slight movement to his right made him look. There was an alcove there, with a desk, a red telephone on it, a chair and a guard. Another plainclothes policeman-type, this time in shirtsleeves, with a revolver worn openly in a shoulder-holster. He nodded to Nick, but didn't smile or speak.

"On to the next door, please," said Hodgeman.

Nick nodded back to the guard and continued down the concrete corridor, his footsteps echoing just out of time with Hodgeman's. Behind him, he heard the faint 'ting' of a telephone being taken off its cradle and then the low voice of the guard, his words indistinguishable.

The procedure with the eyehole was repeated at the next door. There were two policemen behind this one, in a larger and better-appointed alcove. They had upholstered chairs and a leather-topped desk, though it had clearly seen better days.

Hodgeman nodded to the guards, who nodded back with slow deliberation. Nick smiled, but got no smile in return.

"Through the left door, please," said Hodgeman, pointing. There were two doors to choose from, both of unappealing, unmarked steel, bordered with lines of knuckle-sized rivets.

Nick started to push the door but it swung open before he exerted any pressure. There was a much more cheerful room beyond, very much like Nick's tutor's study at Sunbere, with four big leather club-chairs facing a desk, and off to one side, a drinks cabinet with a large black-enamelled radio sitting on top of it. There were three men standing around the cabinet.

The closest was a tall, expensively-dressed vacant-looking man with ridiculous sideburns who Nick recognised as Dorrance; the second-closest a fifty-ish man in a hearty tweed coat with leather patches, the skin of his thick neck hanging over his collar and his fat face much too big for the half-moon glasses that perched on his nose. Lurking behind these two was a nondescript, vaguely unhealthy-looking shorter man who wore exactly the same kind of suit as Hodgeman in a much more untidy way, so he looked nothing like a policeman, serving or otherwise.

"Ah, here is Mr Nicholas Sayre," said Dorrance. He stepped forward, shook Nick's hand and ushered him to the centre of the room. "I'm Dorrance. Good of you to help us out. This is Professor Lackridge, who looks after all our scientific researches."

The fat-faced man extended his hand and shook Nick's with little enthusiasm but a crushing grip. Somewhere in the very distant past, Nick surmised, Professor Lackridge must have been a Rugby enthusiast. Or perhaps a boxer. Now sadly run to fat, but the muscle was still there underneath.

"And this is Mr Malthan, who is... an independent advisor on Old Kingdom matters."

Malthan inclined his head and made a faint, repressed gesture with his hands, turning them towards his forehead as if to brush his almost non-existent hair away. There was something about the action that triggered recognition in Nick.

"You're from the Old Kingdom, aren't you?" he asked. It was unusual for anyone from the Old Kingdom to be encountered this far south. Very few travellers could get authorisation from both King Touchstone and the Ancelstierran government to cross the Wall and the Perimeter. Even fewer would come any further south than Bain. They didn't like it as a rule. It didn't feel right, Sam had always said.

But then this little man didn't have the Charter mark on his forehead, which might make it more bearable for him to be this side of the Wall. Nick instinctively brushed his dark forelock aside to show his Charter mark, his fingers running across it. The mark was quiescent under his touch, showing no sign of its connection to the magical powers of the Old Kingdom.

Malthan clearly saw the mark, even if the others didn't. He stepped a little closer to Nick and spoke in a breathy, half-whine.

"I'm a trader, out of Belisaere," he said. "I've always done a bit of business with some folks in Bain, as my father did before me, and his father before him. We've a Permission from the King, and a Permit from your government. I only come down here every now and then when I've got something special-like that I know Mr Dorrance's lot will be interested in, same as my old dad did for Mr Dorrance's grandad—"

"And we pay very well for what we're interested in, Mr Malthan," interrupted Dorrance. "Don't we?"

"Yes, sir, you do. Only I don't—"

"Malthan has been very useful," interjected Professor Lackridge. "Though we must discount many of his, ahem, traveller's tales. Fortunately he tends to bring us interesting artefacts in addition to his more colourful observations."

"I've always spoken true," said Malthan. "As this young man can tell you. He has the mark and all. He knows."

"Yes, the forehead brand of that cult," remarked Lackridge, with an uninterested glance at Nick's forehead and the mark now mostly concealed once more under his floppy forelock. "Sociologically interesting, of course. Particularly its regrettable prevalence amongst our

Northern Perimeter Reconaissance Unit. I trust it is only an affectation in your case, young man? You haven't gone native on us?"

"It isn't just a religious thing," Nick said carefully. "The Mark is more of a... a connection with... how can I explain... unseen powers. Magic—"

"Yes, yes. I am sure it seems like magic to you," said Lackridge. "But the great majority of it is easily explained as mass hallucination, influence of drugs, hysteria and so forth. It is the minority of events that defy explanation but leave clear physical effects that we are interested in."

"Such as the explosion at Forwin Mill," continued Lackridge. He looked over his half-moon glasses at Nicholas.

Dorrance looked at him as well, his stare suddenly intense.

"Our studies there indicate that the blast was roughly equivalent to the detonation of 20,000 tons of nitrocellulose," continued Lackridge. He rapped his knuckles on the desk as he exclaimed, "Twenty thousand tons! We know of nothing capable of delivering such explosive force, particularly as the bomb itself was reported to be two metallic hemispheres, each no more than ten feet in diameter. Is that right, Nicholas?"

Nick swallowed, his throat moving in a dry gulp. He could feel sweat forming on his forehead and a familiar jangling pain in his right arm and chest.

"I... I don't really know," he said after several long seconds. "I was very ill. Feverish. But it wasn't a bomb. It was the Destroyer. Not something our science can explain. That was my mistake. I thought I could explain everything, under our natural laws, our science. I was wrong."

"You're tired, and clearly still somewhat unwell," said Dorrance. His tone was kindly, but the warmth did not reach his eyes. "We have many more questions, of course, but they can wait until the morning. Professor, why don't you show Nicholas around the establishment. Let him get his bearings. Then back upstairs, and we can all resume life as normal, what? Which reminds me, Nicholas, that everything discussed down here is absolutely confidential. Even the existence of this facility must not be mentioned once you return to the main house. Naturally you will see me, Professor Lackridge and others at dinner, but in our public roles. Most of the guests have no idea that Department Thirteen lurks beneath their feet and we want it to remain that way. I trust you won't have a problem keeping our existence all to yourself?"

"No, not at all," muttered Nick. Inside he was wondering how he could avoid answering questions but still get his pass to cross the Perimeter. Lackridge obviously didn't believe in Old Kingdom magic, which was no great surprise. After all, Nick had been like that himself. But Dorrance had neither voiced such scepticism, or shown it by his body language. Nick definitely did not want to discuss the Destroyer and its nature with anyone who might seriously look into what it was or what had happened at Forwin Mill.

He didn't want to dabble in anything to do with Old Kingdom magic without proper instruction, even two hundred miles south of the Wall.

"Follow me," said Lackridge. "You too, Malthan. I want to show you something related to those photographic plates you found for us."

"I need to get my train," muttered Malthan. "My horses... stabled near Bain... the expense... I'm eager to return home."

"We'll pay you a little extra," said Dorrance, the tone of his voice making it clear Malthan had no choice. "I want Lackridge to see your reaction to one of the artefacts we've picked up. I'll see you at dinner, Nicholas."

Dorrance shook Nick's hand, gave a dismissive wave to Lackridge and ignored Malthan completely. As he turned back to his desk, Nick noticed a paperweight sitting on top of the wooden in-tray. A lump of broken stone etched with intricate symbols. They did not shine or move about, not so far from the Old Kingdom, but Nick recognised their nature, though he did not know their dormant power or meaning. They were Charter marks. The stone itself looked like it had been broken from a greater whole.

Nick looked at Dorrance again and decided that even if it meant having to work out some other way to get across the Perimeter, he was not going to answer any of Dorrance's questions. Or rather, he would answer them vaguely and badly, and generally behave like a well-meaning fool.

Hedge had been an Ancelstierran originally, Nick remembered, as he followed Malthan and the professor out. Dorrance struck him as someone who might be tempted to walk a similar path to Hedge's.

They left through the door Nick had come in, out through the opposite door, and then rapidly through a confusing maze of short corridors and identical riveted metal doors.

"Bit confusing down here, what?" remarked Lackridge. "Takes a while to get your bearings. Dorrance's father built the original tunnels for his underground railway. Modelled on the Corvere Metro, including the lines that never got built in the real thing. But the tunnels have been extended even further since then. We're just going to take a look at our holding area for objects brought in from north of the Wall, or found on our side, near it."

"You mentioned photographic plates," said Nick. "Surely no photographic equipment works over the Wall?"

"That is yet to be properly tested," said Lackridge dismissively. "In any case, these are prints from negative glass plates taken in Bain of a book that was brought across the Wall."

"What kind of book?" Nick asked Malthan.

Malthan looked at Nick, but his eyes failed to meet the younger man's gaze. "The photographs were taken by a former associate of mine. I didn't know she had this book. It burnt of its own accord only minutes after the photographs were captured. Half the plates also melted before I could get them far enough south."

"What was the title of the book?" asked Nick. "And why 'former' associate?"

"She burnt with that b-book," whispered Malthan with a shiver. "I do not know its name. I do not know where Raliese might have got it."

"You see the problems we have to deal with," said Lackridge with a sneer at Malthan. "He probably bought the plates at a school fête in Bain. But they are interesting. The book was some kind of bestiary. We can't read the text as yet, but there are very fine etchings — illustrations of the beasts."

The professor stopped to unlock the next door with a large brass key, but he only opened it a fraction. He turned to Malthan and Nick and said, "The photographs are important as we already had independent evidence that at least one of the beasts depicted in that book really does exist — or existed at one time — in the Old Kingdom."

"Independent evidence of one of those things?" squeaked Malthan. "What kind of—"

"This," declared Lackridge, opening the door wide. "A mummified specimen!"

The storeroom beyond was cluttered with boxes, chests and paraphernalia. For a second, Nick's eye was drawn by two very large blown-up photographs of Forwin Loch that were leaning on the wall near the door. One showed a scene of industry from the last century, and the other showed the destruction wrought by Orannis.

But the big photographs did not hold his attention for more than a moment. There could be no question what Lackridge was referring to. In the middle of the room there was a glass cylinder about nine feet high and five feet in diameter. Inside the case, propped up against a steel frame, was a nightmare.

It looked vaguely human, in the sense that it had a head, a torso, two arms and two legs. But its skin or hide was of a strange violet hue, cross-hatched with lines like a crocodile's, and looked very rough. Its legs were jointed backwards and ended in hooked hooves. The creature's arms stretched down almost to the floor of the case, and ended not in hands, but in club-like appendages that were covered in inch-long barbs. Its torso was thin and cylindrical, rather like that of a wasp. Its head was the most human part, save that it sat on a neck that was twice as long, it had narrow slits instead of ears, and its black, lilac-pupilled eyes — presumably glass made by a skilful taxidermist — were pear-shaped and took up half its face. Its mouth, twice the width of any human's, was almost closed, but Nick could see teeth gleaming there.

Black teeth that shone like polished jet.

"No!" screamed Malthan. He ran back down the corridor, as far as the previous door, which was locked. He beat on the metal with his fists, the drumming echoing down the corridor.

Nick pushed Lackridge gently aside with a quiet "Excuse me." He could feel his heart pounding in his chest, but it was not from fear. It was excitement. The excitement of discovery, of learning something new. The feeling he had always enjoyed, but had been lost to him ever since he'd dug up the metal spheres of the Destroyer.

He leaned forward to touch the case and felt a strange, electric thrill run through his fingers and out along his thumbs. At the same time, there was a stabbing pain in his forehead, strong enough to make him step back and press two fingers hard between his eyes.

"Not a bad specimen," said Lackridge. He spoke conversationally, but he had come very close to Nick and was watching him intently. "Its history is a little murky, but it's been in the country for at least three hundred years, and in the Corvere Bibliomanse for the past thirty-five. One of the things my staff has been doing here at Department Thirteen is cross-indexing all the various institutional records, looking for artefacts and information about our northern neighbours. When we got Malthan's photographs, Dorrance happened to remember he'd seen an actual specimen of one of the creatures before somewhere, as a child. I cross-checked the records at the Bibliomanse, found the thing, and we had it brought up here."

Nick nodded absently. The pain in his head was receding. It appeared to emanate from his Charter mark, though that should be totally quiescent this far from the Wall. Unless there was a roaring gale blowing down from the north, which he supposed might have happened since he came down into Department Thirteen's subterranean lair. It was impossible to tell what was going on in the world above them.

"Apparently the thing was found about ten miles on our side of the Wall, wrapped in three chains," continued Lackridge. "One of silver, one of lead, and one made from braided daisies. That's what the notes say, though of course we don't have the chains to prove it. If there was a silver one it must have been worth a pretty penny. Long before the Perimeter, of course, so it was some time before the authorities got hold of it. The local folk wanted to drag it back to the Wall, according to the records, but fortunately there was a visiting Captain Inquirer who had it shipped south. Should never have got rid of the Captain Inquirers. Wouldn't have minded being one myself. Don't suppose anyone would bring them back now. Lily-livered lot, the present government... excepting your uncle of course..."

"My father also sits in the Moot," said Nick. "On the government benches."

"Well, of course, everyone says my politics are to the right of old Arbiter Werris Blue-Nose, so don't mind me," said Lackridge. He stepped back into the corridor and shouted, "Come back here, Mr Malthan. It won't bite you!"

As Lackridge spoke, Nick thought he saw the creature's eyes move. Just a fraction, but there was a definite sense of movement. With it, all his sense of excitement was banished in a second, to be replaced by a growing fear.

It's alive, thought Nick.

He stepped back to the door, almost knocking over Lackridge, his mind working furiously.

The thing is alive. Quiescent. Conserving its energies, so far from the Old Kingdom. It must be some Free Magic creature, and it's just waiting for a chance...

"Thank you, Professor Lackridge, but I find myself suddenly rather keen on a cup of tea," blurted Nick. "Do you think we might come back and look at this speciment tomorrow?"

"I'm supposed to make Malthan touch the case," said Lackridge. "Dorrance was most insistent upon it. Wants to see his reaction."

Nick edged back and looked down the corridor. Malthan was still crouched by the door.

"I think you've seen his reaction," he said. "Anything more would simply be cruel, and hardly scientific."

"He's only an Old Kingdom trader," said Lackridge. "He's not even strictly legal. No visa. We can do whatever we like with him."

"What!" exclaimed Nick.

"Within reason," Lackridge added hastily. "I mean, nothing too drastic. Do him good."

"I think he needs to get on a train north and back to the Old Kingdom," said Nick firmly. He was liking Lackridge less and less with every passing minute, and the whole

Department Thirteen set up seemed very dubious. It was all very well for his Uncle Edward to talk about having extra-legal entities to do things the government could not, but the line had to be drawn somewhere and Nick didn't think Dorrance or Lackridge knew where to draw it, or if they did, when not to step over it.

"I'll just see how he is," added Nick. An idea started to rise up from the recesses of his mind as he walked down the corridor towards the crouched and shivering man pressed against the door. "Perhaps we can walk out together."

"Mr Dorrance was most insistent—"

"I'm sure he won't mind if you tell him that I insisted on escorting Malthan on his way."

"But—"

"I am insisting, you know," cut in Nick forcefully. "As it is I shall have a few words to say about this place to my uncle."

"If you're going to be like that, I don't think I have any choice," said Lackridge petulantly. "We were assured that you would fully cooperate with our research."

"*I* will cooperate, but I don't think Malthan needs to do any more for Department Thirteen," said Nick. He bent down and helped the Old Kingdom trader up. He was surprised by how much the smaller man was shaking. He seemed totally in the grip of panic, though he calmed a little when Nick took his arm above the elbow. "Now, please show us out. And you can organise someone to take Malthan to the railway station."

"You don't understand the importance of our work," said Lackridge. "Or our methods. Observing the superstitious reactions of Northerners and our own people delivers legitimate and 'potentially useful information."

This was clearly only a pro forma protest, because as Lackridge spoke he unlocked the door and led them quickly through the corridors. After a few minutes, Nick found that he didn't need to half carry Malthan any more, but just point him in the right direction.

Eventually, after numerous turns and more doors that required laborious unlocking, they came to a double-width steel door with no less than two peepholes. Lackridge knocked, and after a brief inspection they were admitted to a guardroom inhabited by five policeman-types. Four were sitting around a linoleum-topped table under a single suspended light bulb, drinking tea and eating doorstop-sized sandwiches. Hodgeman was the fifth, clearly still on duty as, unlike the others, he had not removed his coat.

"Sergeant Hodgeman," Lackridge called out rather too loudly, "please escort Mr Sayre upstairs and have one of your other officers take Malthan to Dorrance Halt and see he gets on the next northbound train."

"Very good, sir," replied Hodgeman. He hesitated for a moment, then with a curiously unpleasant emphasis that Nick would have missed if he wasn't paying careful attention, he said, "Constable Ripton, you see to Malthan."

"Just a moment," said Nick. "I've had a thought. Malthan can take a message from me over to my uncle, the Chief Minister, at the Golden Sheaf. Then someone from his staff can take Malthan on to the nearest station."

"One of my men would happily take a message for you, sir," said Sergeant Hodgeman. "And Dorrance Halt is much closer than the Golden Sheaf. That's all of twenty mile away."

"Thank you," said Nick, "but I want the Chief Minister to hear Malthan directly about some matters relating to the Old Kingdom. That won't be a problem, will it? Malthan, I'll just write something out for you to take to Garran, my uncle's principal secretary."

Nick took out his pocketbook and gold propelling pencil, and casually leaned against the wall. The five policeman watched him with studied disinterest masking hostility, Lackridge with more open aggression, and Malthan with the sad eyes of the doomed.

Nick began to whistle tunelessly through his teeth, pretending to be oblivious to the pent-up institutional aggression focused upon him. He wrote quickly, sighed and pretended to cross out what he'd written, ripped out the page, palmed it and started to write again.

"Very hard to concentrate the mind in these underground chambers of yours," Nick said to Lackridge. "I don't know how you get anything done. Expect you've got cockroaches too... maybe rats... I mean, what's that?"

He pointed with the pencil. Only Malthan and Lackridge turned to look. The policemen kept up their steady stare. Nick stared back, but he felt a slight fear begin to swim about his stomach. Surely they wouldn't risk doing anything to Edward Sayre's nephew? And yet... they were clearly planning to imprison Malthan at the least, or perhaps something worse. Nick wasn't going to let that happen.

"Only a shadow, but I bet you do have rats. Stands to reason. Underground. Tea and biscuits about," said Nick, as he ripped out the second page. He folded it, wrote 'Mr Thomas Garran' on the outside and handed it to Malthan, at the same time stepping across to shield his next action from everyone except Lackridge, who he stumbled against.

"Oh, sorry!" he exclaimed, and in that moment of apparently lost balance, slid the palmed first note into Malthan's still open hand.

"I... ah... still not quite recovered from the events at Forwin Mill," Nick mumbled, as Lackridge suppressed an oath and jumped back.

The policemen had stepped forward, but it seemed only to catch him if he fell. Sergeant Hodgeman had seen him stumble before. They were clearly suspicious, but didn't know what he had done. He hoped.

"Bit unsteady on my pins," continued Nick. "Nothing to do with drink, unfortunately. That might make it seem worthwhile. Now I must get on upstairs and dress for dinner. Who's taking Malthan over to the Golden Sheaf?"

"I am, sir. Constable Ripton."

"Very good, constable. I trust you'll have a pleasant evening drive. I'll telephone ahead to make sure that Uncle's staff are expecting you and have dinner laid on."

"Thank you, sir," said Ripton woodenly. Again, if Nick hadn't been paying careful attention he might have missed the young constable flick his eyes up and down, and then twice towards Sergeant Hodgeman. A twitch Nick interpreted as a call for help from the junior police officer, looking for Hodgeman to tell him how to satisfy his immediate masters as well as insure himself against the interference of any greater authority.

"Get on with it then, constable," said Hodgeman, his words as ambiguous as his expression.

"Let's all get upstairs," Nick declared with false cheer he dredged up from somewhere. "After you, Sergeant. Malthan, if you wouldn't mind walking with me I'll see you to your car. Got a couple of questions about the Old Kingdom I'm sure you can answer."

"Anything, anything," babbled Malthan. He came so close Nick thought the little trader was going to hug him. "Let us get out from under the earth. With that—"

"Yes, I agree," interrupted Nick. He gestured at the door and met Sergeant Hodgeman's stare. All the policemen moved closer. Casual steps. A foot slid forward here, a diagonal pace towards Nick.

Lackridge coughed something that might have been "Dorrance," scuttled to the door leading back to the tunnels, opened it just wide enough to admit his bulk, and squeezed through. Nick thought about calling him back, but instantly dismissed the idea. He didn't want to show any weakness.

But with Lackridge gone, there was no longer a witness. Nick knew Malthan didn't count, not to anyone in Department Thirteen.

Sergeant Hodgeman pushed one heavy booted foot forward and advanced on Nick and Malthan, till his face was inches away from Nick's. It was an intimidating posture, long beloved of sergeants, and Nick knew it well from his days in the school cadets.

Hodgeman didn't say anything. He just stared, a fierce stare that Nick realised hid a mind calculating how far he could go to keep Malthan captive, and what he might be able to do to Nicholas Sayre, without causing greater trouble.

"My uncle, the Chief Minister," whispered Nick, very softly. "My father, a member of the Moot. Marshal Harngorm is my mother's uncle. My second cousin the Hereditary Arbiter himself."

"As you say, sir," said Hodgeman loudly. He stepped back, the sound of his heel on the concrete snapping through the tension that had risen in the room. "I'm sure you know what you're doing."

That was a warning of consequences to come, Nick knew. But he didn't care. He wanted to save Malthan, but most of all at that moment he wanted to get out under the sun again. He wanted to stand above ground, and put as much earth and concrete and as many locked doors as possible between himself and the creature in the case.

Yet even when the afternoon sunlight was softly warming his face, Nick wasn't much comforted. He watched Constable Ripton and Malthan leave in a small green van that looked exactly like the sort of vehicle that would be used to dispose of a body in a moving picture about the fictional Department Thirteen. Then, while lurking near the footmen's side door, he saw several gleaming, expensive cars drive up to disgorge their gleaming, expensive passengers. He recognised most of the guests. None were friends. They were all people he would formerly have described as frivolous and now he just didn't care about at all. Even the beautiful young women failed to make more than a momentary impact. His mind was elsewhere.

Nick was thinking about Malthan and the two messages he carried. One, the obvious one, was addressed to Thomas Garran, Uncle Edward's principal private secretary. It said:

> Garran
> Uncle will want to talk to the bearer
> (Malthan, an Old Kingdom trader) for five
> minutes or so. Please ensure he is then
> escorted to the Perimeter by Foxe's people or
> Captain Sverenson's, not D13. Ask Uncle to
> call me urgently. Word of a Sayre. Nicholas.

The second, more hastily scrawled, said:

> Send telegram TO MAGISTRIX WYVERLEY
> COLLEGE NICK FOUND BAD KINGDOM
> CREATURE DORRANCE HALL TELL
> ABHORSEN HELP.

There was every possibility that neither message would get through, Nick thought. It would all depend on what Dorrance and his minions thought they could get away with. And that depended on what they thought they could do to one Nicholas Sayre before he caused them too much trouble.

Nick shivered and went back inside. As he expected, when he asked to use a telephone, the footman referred him to the butler, who was very apologetic and bowed several times while regretting that the line was down and probably would not be fixed for several days, the telegraph company being notoriously slow in the country.

With that avenue cut off, Nick retreated to his room, ostensibly to dress for dinner. In practice, he spent most of the time writing a report to his uncle and another telegram to the Magistrix at Wyverley College. He hid the report in the lining of his suitcase and went in search of a particular valet who he knew must have come with one of the guests he had seen arrive, the ageing dandy Hericourt Danjers. The permanent staff of Dorrance Hall would all really be Department Thirteen agents or informants at the least, but it was much less likely the guests' servants would be.

Danjer's valet was famous among servants for his ability with bootblack, champagne and a secret oil. So neither he nor anyone else in the below-stairs parlour were much surprised when the Chief Minister's nephew sought him out with a pair of shoes in hand. The valet was a little more surprised to find a note inside the shoes asking him to go out to the village and secretly send a telegram, but as the note was wrapped around four double-guinea pieces, he was happy to do so. When he'd finished his duties, of course.

Back in his room, Nick hastily dressed. He tied his bow tie slowly, his hands moving automatically as he wondered what else he should be doing. All kinds of plans raced through his head, only to be abandoned as impractical, or foolish, or likely to make matters worse.

With his tie finally done, Nick went to his case and took out a large leather wallet. There were three things inside. Two were letters, both written neatly on thick, linen-rich handmade paper, but in markedly different hands.

The first letter was from Nick's old friend, Prince Sameth. It was concerned primarily with Sam's current projects and was illustrated in the margins with small diagrams. From the letter, Sam's time was being spent almost entirely on the fabrication and enchantment of a replacement hand for Lirael, and the planning and design of a fishing hut on an island in the Ratterlin Delta. Sam did not explain why he wanted to build a fishing hut, and Nick had not had a reply to his most recent letter seeking enlightenment. This was not unusual. Sam was an infrequent correspondent, and there was no regular mail service of any kind between Ancelstierre and the Old Kingdom.

Nick didn't bother to read Sam's letter again. He put it aside and carefully unfolded the second letter, and read it for the hundredth or two hundredth time, hoping that this time he would uncover some hidden meaning in the innocuous words.

This letter was from Lirael, and it was quite short. The writing was so regular, so perfectly spaced and so free of ink-splotches that Nick wondered if it had been copied from a rough version. If it had, what did that mean? Did Lirael always make fine copies of her letters? Or had she done it just for him?

Dear Nick

I trust you are recovering well. I am much better, and Sam says my new hand will be ready soon. Ellimere has been teaching me to play tennis, a game from your country, but I really do need two hands. I have also started to work with the Abhorsen. Sabriel, I mean, though I still find it hard to call her that. I still laugh when I remember you calling her "Mrs Abhorsen Ma'am Sir". I was surprised by that laugh, amidst such sorrow and pain. It was a strange day, wasn't it? Waiting for everything to be discussed and sorted and explained just enough so we could all go home, with the two of us lying side by side on our stretchers with so much going on all around. You made it better for me, telling me about my friend the Disreputable Dog. I am very grateful for that. That is why I'm writing, really, and Sam said he was sending something so this could go in with it.

Be well.
Lirael,
Abhorsen-in-Waiting and Remembrancer

Nick stared at the letter for several minutes after he finished reading it, then gently folded it and returned it to the wallet. He drew out the third thing, which had come in a package with the letters three weeks ago, though it had apparently left the Old Kingdom at least a month before that. It was a small, very plain dagger, the blade and hilt blued steel, with brass wire wound around the grip, the pommel just a big teardrop of metal.

Sam held it up to the light. He could see faint etched symbols upon the blade, but that's all they were. Faint, etched symbols. Not living, moving Charter marks, bright and flowing, all gold and sunshine. That's what Charter-spelled swords normally looked like, the marks leaping and splashing across the metal.

Nick knew he ought to be comforted. If the Charter marks on his dagger were still and dead, then the thing beneath the house should be as well. But he knew it wasn't. He'd seen its eyes flicker.

There was a knock on the door. Nick hastily put the dagger back in its sheath.

"Yes!" he called. The sheathed dagger was still in his hand. For a moment he considered exchanging it for the slim .32 automatic pistol in his suitcase's outer pocket. But he decided against it when the person at the door called out to him.

"Nicholas Sayre?"

It was a woman's voice. A young woman's voice, with the hint of a laugh in it. Not a servant. One of the beautiful young women he'd seen arrive. Probably a not very successful actor or a singer, the usual adornments of typical country house parties.

"Yes. Who is it?"

"Tesrya. Don't say you don't remember me. Perhaps a glimpse will remind you. Let me in. I've got a bottle of champagne. I thought we might have a drink before dinner."

Nick didn't remember her, but that didn't mean anything. He knew she would have singled him out from the seating plan for dinner, homing in on the surname 'Sayre'. He supposed he should at least tell her to go away to her face. Courtesy to women, even fortune-hunters, had been drummed into him all his life.

"Just one drink?"

Nick hesitated, then tucked the sheathed dagger down the inside of his trousers, at the hip. He held his foot against the door in case he needed to shut it in a hurry, turned the key and opened it a fraction.

He had the promised glimpse. Pale, melancholy eyes in a very white face, a forced smile from too-red lips. But there were also two hooded men there. One threw his shoulder against the door to keep it open. The other grabbed Nick by the hair and pushed a pad the size of a small pillow against his face.

Nick tried not to breathe as he threw himself backwards, losing some hair in the process, but the sickly sweet smell of chloroform was already in his mouth and nose. The two men gave him no time to recover his balance. One pushed him back to the foot of the bed, while the other got his right arm in a wrestling hold. Nick struck out with his left, but his fist wouldn't go where he wanted it to. His arm felt like a rubbery length of pipe, the elbow gone soft.

Nick kept flailing, but the pad was back on his mouth and nose, and all his senses started to shatter into little pieces like a broken mosaic. He couldn't make sense of what he saw and heard and felt and all he could smell was a sickly scent like a cheap perfume badly imitating the scent of flowers.

In another few seconds, he was unconscious.

Nicholas Sayre returned to his senses very slowly. It was like waking up drunk after a party, his mind still clouded and a hangover building in his head and stomach. It was dark and he was disorientated. He tried to move, and for a frightened instant thought he was paralysed. Then he felt restraints at his wrists and ankles, and a hard surface under his head and back. He was tied to a table, or perhaps a hard bench.

"Ah, the mind wakes," said a voice in the darkness. Nick thought for a second, his clouded mind slowly processing the sound. He knew that voice. Dorrance.

"Would you like to see what is happening?" asked Dorrance. Nick heard him take a few steps, heard the click of a rotary electric switch. Harsh light came with the click, so bright Nick had to screw his eyes shut, tears instantly welling up in the corners.

"Look, Mr Sayre. Look at your most useful work."

Nick slowly opened his eyes. At first all he could see was a naked, very bright electric globe swinging directly above his head. Blinking to clear the tears, he looked to one side.

Dorrance was there, leaning against the concrete wall. He smiled and pointed to the other side, his hand held close against his chest, fist clenched, index finger extended.

Nick rolled his head over and recoiled, straining against the ropes that bound his ankles, thighs and wrists to a steel operating table with raised rails.

The creature from the case was right next to him. No longer in the case, but stretched out on an adjacent table ten inches lower than Nick's. It was not tied up. There was a red rubber tube running from Nick's wrist to a metal stand next to the creature's head. The tube ended an inch above the monster's slightly open mouth. Blood was dripping from the tube, small dark blobs falling in between its jet black teeth.

Nick's blood.

Nick struggled furiously for another second, panic building in every muscle. The ropes did not give at all, and the tube was not dislodged. Then, his strength exhausted, he stopped.

"You need not be concerned, Mr Nicholas Sayre," said Dorrance. He moved around to look at the creature, gently tapping Nick's feet as he passed. "I am only taking a pint. This will all just be a nightmare in the morning, half-remembered, with a dozen men swearing to your conspicuous consumption of brandy."

As he spoke, the light above him suddenly flared into white-hot brilliance. Then, with a bang, the bulb exploded into powder and the room went dark. Nick blinked, the after-image of the filament burning a white line across the room. But even with that, he could see another light. Two violet sparks that were faint at first, but became brighter and more intense.

Nick recognised them instantly as the creature's eyes. At the same time, he smelt a sudden, acrid odour, that got stronger and stronger, coating the back of his mouth and making his nostrils burn. A metallic stench that he knew only too well.

The smell of Free Magic.

The violet eyes moved suddenly, jerking up. Nick felt the rubber hose suddenly pulled from his wrist, and the wet feel of blood dripping down his hand.

He still couldn't see anything, save the creature's eyes. They moved again, very quickly, as the thing stood up and crossed the room. It ignored Nick, though he struggled violently against his bonds as it went past. He couldn't see what happened next, but something... or someone... was hurled against his table, the impact rocking it almost to the point of toppling over.

"No!" shouted Dorrance. "Don't go out! I'll bring you blood! Whatever kind you need—"

There was a tearing sound, and flickering light suddenly filled the room. Nick saw the creature silhouetted in the doorway, holding the heavy door it had just ripped from its steel hinges. It threw this aside and strode out into the corridor, lifting its head back to emit a hissing shriek that was so high-pitched it made Nick's ears ring.

Dorrance staggered after it for a moment, then returned and flung open a cabinet on the wall. As he picked up the telephone handset inside, the lights in the corridor fizzed and went out.

Nick heard the dial spin three times. Then Dorrance swore and tapped the receiver before dialling again. This time the phone worked and he spoke, very quickly.

"Hello? Lackridge? Can you hear me? Yes... ignore the crackle. Is Hodgeman there? Tell him 'Situation Dora.' All the fire doors must be barred and the exit grilles activated. No, tell him now ... 'Dora' ... Yes, yes. It worked, all too well. She's completely active, and I heard her clearly for the first time, wide awake! Sayre's blood was too rich, and there's something wrong with it. She needs to dilute it with normal blood... what? Active! Running around! Of course you're in danger! She doesn't care whose blood... we need to keep her in the tunnels, then I'll find someone... one of the servants. Just get on with it!"

Nick kept silent, but he remembered the dagger at his hip. If he could bend his hand back and reach it, he might be able to unsheath it enough to work the rope against the blade. If he didn't bleed to death first.

"So, Mr Sayre," said Dorrance in the darkness. "Why would your blood be different to any other bearer of the Charter mark? It causes me some distress to think I have given her the wrong sort. Not to mention the difficulty that now arises from her desire to wash her drink down."

"I don't know," whispered Nick, after a moment's hesitation. He'd thought of pretending to be unconscious, but Dorrance would certainly test that.

In the distance, muffled by doors, electric bells began a harsh, insistent clangour. At first, none sounded in the corridor outside, then one stuttered into life. At the same time, the light beyond the door flickered on, off and on again, before giving up in a shower of sparks that plunged the room back into total darkness.

Something touched Nick's feet. He flinched, taking off some skin against the ropes. A few seconds later there was a click near his head, the whiff of kerosene, and a four-inch flame suddenly shed some light on the scene. Dorrance lifted his cigarette lighter and set it on a head-high shelf, still burning.

He took a bandage from the same shelf and started to wind it around Nick's wrist.

"Waste not, want not," said Dorrance. "Even if your blood is tainted, it has succeeded beyond my dearest hopes. I have long dreamed of waking Her."

"It, you mean," croaked Nick.

Dorrance tied off the bandage, then suddenly slapped Nick's face hard with the back of his hand.

"You are not worthy to speak of Her! She is a goddess! A goddess! She should never have been sent away! My father was a fool! Fortunately I am not!"

Nick chose silence once more, and waited for another blow. But it didn't come. Dorrance took a deep breath, then bent under the table. Nick craned his head to see what he was doing, but could only hear the rattle of metal on metal.

The man emerged holding two sets of old-style handcuffs, the kind where the cuffs were screwed in rather than key-locked. He quickly handcuffed Nick's left wrist to the metal rail of the bed, then did the same with the second set to his right wrist.

"It has been politic to play the disbeliever about your Charter Magic," he said as he screwed the handcuffs tight. "But She has told me different in my dreams, and if She can rise so far from the Wall, perhaps your magic will also serve you... and ropes do burn or fray so easily. Rest here, young Nicholas. My mistress may soon need a second drink, whether the taste disagrees with her or not."

After shaking the handcuffs to make sure they were secure, Dorrance picked up his still-burning cigarette lighter and left, muttering something to himself that Nick couldn't quite hear. It didn't sound entirely sane, but Nick didn't need to hear bizarre mumblings to know that Dorrance was neither the harmless eccentric of his public image or the cunning spymaster of his secret identity. He was a madman in league with a Free Magic creature.

As soon as Dorrance had gone, Nick tested the handcuffs, straining against them. But he couldn't move his hands more than a few inches off the table, certainly not far enough to reach the screws. However, he could reach the pommel of his dagger with the tips of his three fingers. After a few failed attempts, he managed to get the blade out, and by rolling his body, sliced through the rope on his left wrist, cutting himself slightly in the process.

He was trying to move his left ankle up towards his hand when he heard the first, distant gunshots and screams. There were more, but they got fainter and fainter, lending hope that the creature was moving further away.

Not that it made much difference, Nick thought, as he rattled his handcuffs in frustration. He couldn't get free by himself. He would have to work out a plan to get Dorrance to at least uncuff him when he returned. Then he might be able to surprise him. If he did return. Until then, Nick decided, he should try to rest and gather his strength. As much as the adrenaline coursing through his bloodstream would let him rest, immobilised on a steel operating table in a secret underground facility run by a lunatic, with a totally inimical creature on the loose.

He lay in silence for what he estimated was somewhere between fifteen minutes and a hour, being totally unable to judge the passage of time when he was in the dark and so wound up with tension. In that time, every noise seemed loud and significant, and made him twist and tilt his head, as if by moving his ears he could better capture and identify the sound of what was going on.

There was silence for a while, or near enough to it. Then he heard more gunshots but without the screams. The shots were repeated a few seconds later, louder and closer, and were followed by the slam and echo of metal doors and then hurrying footsteps. More than one person.

"Help!" cried Nick. "Help! I'm tied up in here!"

He figured it was worth calling out. Even fanatical Department Thirteen employees must have realised by now that Dorrance was crazy and he'd unleashed something awful upon them.

"Help!"

The footsteps came closer, and an electric torch beam swung into the room, blinding Nick. Behind its yellow nimbus he saw two silhouettes. One man standing in front of another.

"Get those shackles off and untie him," ordered the man behind. Nick recognised the voice. It was Constable Ripton. The man who shuffled ahead, allowing the light to fall on his face and side, was Professor Lackridge. A pale and trembling Lackridge, who fumbled with the screws of the handcuffs. Ripton was holding a revolver on him, but Nick doubted that was why the scientist was so scared.

"Sorry to take so long, sir," said Ripton calmly. "Bit of a panic going on."

Nick suddenly understood what Ripton had actually been trying to convey with his quick glances aside back in the guardroom. His uncle's words ran through his head.

It is watched over quite carefully, I assure you.

"You're not really D13 are you? You're one of my uncle's men?"

"Yes, sir. Indirectly. I report to Mr Foxe."

Nick sat up as the handcuffs came off and drew his dagger, quickly slicing through the remaining ropes. He was not entirely surprised to see the faint glimmer of Charter marks on the blade, though they were nowhere near as bright and potent as they would be near the Wall.

"Can you walk, sir? We need to get moving."

Nick nodded. He felt a bit light-headed, but otherwise fine, so he guessed he hadn't lost too much blood to the creature.

"Sorry," blurted Lackridge as Nick slid off the table and stood up. "I never... never thought that this would happen. I never believed Dorrance, thought only to humour him... he said that it spoke to him in dreams, and if it was more awake, then... we hoped to be able to discover the secret of waking mental communication... it was—"

"Mind control is what Dorrance thought he could get from it," interrupted Ripton. He tapped his coat pocket. "I've got your diary here. Mind control through people's dreams. And you just went along with whatever Dorrance wanted, you stupid sod."

"What's actually happening?" asked Nick. "Has it killed anyone?"

Lackridge choked out something unintelligible.

"Anyone! It's killed almost everyone down here, and by now it's probably upstairs killing everyone there," said

Ripton. "Guns don't work up close to it, bullets fired further back don't do a thing, and the electric barrier grids just went phht when it walked up! As soon as I figured it was trying to get out, I doubled around behind it. Now I reckon we follow its path out and then run like the clappers while it's busy—"

"We can't do that," said Nick. "What about the guests? And the servants, even if they do work for D13, they can't be abandoned."

"There's nothing we can do," said Ripton. He no longer appeared so calm. "I don't know what that thing is, but I do know that it has already killed a dozen highly-trained and fully-armed D13 operatives. Killed them and... and drank their blood. Not... not something I ever want to see again..."

"I know what it is," said Nick. "Somewhat. It is a Free Magic creature from the Old Kingdom. A source of Free Magic itself, which is why guns and electricity don't work near it. I would have thought that bullets coming in from further away would at least hurt it, though—"

"They bounced off. I saw the lead splashes on its hide... Here's a flashlight. You go in front, professor. Get your key ready."

"We have to try and save the people upstairs," said Nick firmly as they nervously entered the corridor, flashlight beams probing the darkness in both directions. "Has it definitely already got out of here?"

"I don't know! It was through the second guardroom. The library exit might slow it more. It's basically a revolving reinforced concrete and steel slab, like a vault door. Supposed to be bomb-proof—"

"Is there another way up?"

"No," said Ripton.

"Yes," said Lackridge. He stopped and turned, the bronze key gleaming in his hand. Ripton stepped back, and his finger whipped from rest outside the trigger guard to curl directly around the trigger.

"The dumbwaiter!" blurted Lackridge. "Dorrance has a dumbwaiter from the wine cellar below us here, that goes up through his office to the pantry above."

"What time is it?" asked Nick.

"Half-nine," said Ripton. "Or near enough."

"The guests will be at dinner," said Nick. "They won't have heard what's going on down here. If we can take the dumbwaiter to the pantry, we might be able to get everyone out of the house before the creature breaks through to the library."

"And then what?" asked Ripton. "Talk as we go. Head for the office, prof."

"It'd not a Dead thing, so running water won't do much," said Nick as they broke into a jog. "Fire might though... if we made a barrier of hay and set it alight, that could work. It would attract attention at least. Bring help."

"I don't think the sort of help we need exists around here," said Ripton. "I've never been up north, but I know people in the NPRU and this is right up their alley. Things like this just don't happen down here."

"No, they don't," said Nick. "They wouldn't have happened this time, either, only Dorrance fed his creature the wrong blood."

"I don't understand," puffed Lackridge. Now that they were heading for a possible exit he had got more of a grip on himself. "I didn't believe him... but... Dorrance thought the blood of one of you people with the Charter brand would rouse the creature a little, without danger. Then when we got you to come in for the Forwin Blast investigation, he saw you had a Charter mark. The opportunity—"

"Shut up!" ordered Ripton. As Lackridge calmed down, the policeman got more tense.

"Dorrance worships the creature, but I don't think even he wanted it this active," snapped Nick. "I can't explain the whole thing to you, but my blood is infused with Free Magic as well as the Charter. I guess the combination is what got the creature going so strongly... but it was too rich or something, that's why it's trying to dilute it with normal blood... I wonder if that means that the power it got from my blood will run out? Maybe it'll just drop at some point..."

Lackridge shook his head, as if he still couldn't believe what he was hearing, despite the evidence.

"It might come back for a refill from you as well," said Ripton. "That's the office. You first, professor."

"But what if the creature's in there?"

"That's why you're going first," said Ripton. He gestured with his revolver, and when Lackridge still didn't move, pushed him hard with his left hand. The bulky ex-boxer rebounded from the door and stood there, his eyes glazed and jowls shivering.

"Oh, I'll go first!" said Nick. He pushed Lackridge aside a little more gently, turned the door handle and went into Dorrance's office. It was the room he'd been in before, with the big leather club-chairs, the desk and the drinks cabinet.

"It's empty, come on!"

Ripton locked the door after him as they entered the room, and slid the top and bottom bolts home.

"Thought I heard something," he whispered. "Maybe it's coming back. Keep your voices down."

"Where's the dumbwaiter?" asked Nick.

Lackridge crossed to a bookshelf and pressed a corner. The whole shelf swung out an inch, allowing Lackridge to get a grip and open it out completely. The light of Nick's flashlight revealed a small square space behind it about three feet high and wide: a small goods elevator used as a dumbwaiter.

"We'll have to go one at a time," said Ripton. He slipped his revolver into his shoulder holster, laid his torch on the desk, and dragged one of the heavy, studded leather chairs against the door. "You first, Mr Sayre. I think it must have heard us, or smelt us or something, there's definitely—"

"Let me go!" burst out Lackridge, with a dart towards the elevator. He was brought up short as Ripton whirled around and kicked him behind the knee, bringing him crashing down, his fall rattling the bottles in the drinks cabinet.

Nick hesitated, then climbed into the dumbwaiter. There were two buttons on the outside frame of the elevator, marked with up and down arrows, but as he expected, neither did anything. However, there was a hatch in the ceiling which, when pushed open, revealed a vertical shaft and some heavily-greased cables. The shaft was walled with old yellow bricks, and some had been removed every few feet to make irregular but useable hand- and foot-holds.

Nick ducked his head out and said, "It's electric, not working. We'll have to climb the—"

His voice was drowned out as the metal door suddenly rang like a bell and the middle of it bowed in, struck with tremendous force from the other side.

"Fire!" shouted Nick as he jumped out of the elevator. "Start a fire against the door!"

He rushed to the drinks cabinet and ripped it open as the creature struck the door again. This second blow sheared the bolt and bent the top half of the door over, and a dark shape with glowing violet eyes could be seen beyond the doorway. At the same time, Ripton's electric torch shone intensely bright for a second, then went out for ever.

The remaining flashlight, left in the elevator, continued to shine erratically, as Nick frantically threw whisky and gin bottles at the base of the door, and Ripton struck a match on the chair leg, swearing as it burst into splinters instead of flame. Then his second match flared and he flicked it across to the alcohol-soaked chair; there was a blue flash and a ball of flame exploded around the door, searing off both Ripton's and Nick's eyebrows.

The creature made a horrid gargling, drowning sound and backed away. Nick and Ripton retreated to the wall and hunched down to try and get below the smoke which was already filling the room. Lackridge was still slumped on the floor, not moving, the smoke twirling and curling over his back.

"Go!" coughed Ripton, gesturing with his thumb at the dumbwaiter.

"What... about... ridge?"

"Leave him!"

"You go!"

Ripton shook his head, but when Nick crawled across to Lackridge, he climbed into the dumbwaiter. The big man was a dead weight, too heavy for Nick to move without standing up. An unopened bottle exploded behind him as he tried again, showering the back of his neck with hot glass. The smoke was getting thicker with every second, and the heat more intense.

"Get up!" coughed Nick. "You'll die here!"

Lackridge didn't move.

Flames licked at Nick's back and he smelt burning hair. He could do nothing more for the professor. He had only reduced his own chances of survival. Cradling his arms around his head, Nick dived into the dumbwaiter.

He had hoped for clean air there, but it was no better. The elevator shaft was acting as a chimney, sucking up the smoke. Nick felt his throat and lungs closing up, and his arms and legs growing weaker. He thrust himself through the hatch and climbed on to the roof of the dumbwaiter and felt about for the hatch cover, slapping it down in the hope that this might stop some of the smoke. Then, coughing and spitting, he felt for the handholds and began to climb.

Somewhere up above him he could hear Ripton, coughing and swearing. But Nick wasn't listening for Ripton. All his senses were attuned to what might be happening lower down. Would the creature come through the fire and swarm up the shaft?

The smoke did begin to thin a little as Nick climbed, but it was still thick enough for him to smash his head into Ripton's boots after he had climbed up about forty feet. The sudden shout it provoked confirmed that Ripton had been thinking about where the creature was as well.

"Sorry!" gasped Nick. "I don't think it's following us."

"There's a door here, I'm standing on the foot of it, but I can't slide the bloody thing— got it!"

Light spilled into the shaft as smoke wafted out of it. Hard, white gaslight. Ripton stepped through, then turned to help Nick pull himself up and over.

They were in a long, whitewashed room lined from floor to ceiling with shelves and shelves of packaged food of all varieties. Tins and boxes and packets and sacks and bottles and puncheons and jars.

There was a door at the other end. It was open, and a white-clad cook's assistant was staring at them open-mouthed.

"Fire!" shouted Nick, waving his arms to clear the smoke that was billowing out fast from behind him. He started to walk forward, continuing to half-shout, his voice raspy and dulled by smoke. "Fire in the cellars! Everyone needs to get out, on to the... which field is closest, with hay?"

"The home meadow," croaked Ripton. He cleared his throat and tried again. "The home meadow."

"Tell the staff to evacuate the house and assemble on the home meadow," ordered Nick, in his most commanding manner. "I will tell the guests."

"Yes, sir!" stammered the cook's assistant. There was still a lot of smoke coming out now, even though Ripton had managed to close the door. "Cook will be angry!"

"Hurry up!" said Nick. He strode past the assistant and along a short corridor, to find himself in the main kitchen, where half a dozen immaculately white-clad men were engaged in an orderly but complex dance around a number of benches and stove tops, directed by the rapid snap of commands from a small, thin man with the tallest and whitest hat.

"Fire!" roared Nick. "Get out to the home meadow! Fire!"

He repeated this as he strode through the kitchen and out of the swinging doors immediately after a waiter, who showed the excellence of his training by hardly looking behind him for more than a second.

As Nick had thought, the guests at dinner were making enough noise of their own that they would never have heard any kind of commotion deep in the earth under their feet. Even when he burst out of the servant's corridor and jumped on to the empty chair that was probably his near the head of the table, only five or six of the forty guests looked around.

Then Ripton fired two rapid shots into the ceiling.

"Ladies and gentleman, I do beg your pardon!" shouted Nick. "There is a fire in the house! Please get up at once and follow Mr Ripton here to the home meadow!"

Silence met this announcement for perhaps half a second, then Nick was assaulted with questions, comments and laughter. It was such a babble that he could hardly make out any one coherent stream of words, but clearly half the guests thought this was some game of Dorrance's; a quarter of them wanted to go and get their jewels, favourite coats or lapdogs; and the other quarter intended to keep eating and drinking no matter whether the house burnt down around them or not.

"This isn't a joke!" screamed Nick, his voice barely penetrating the hubbub. "If you don't go now you'll be dead in fifteen minutes! Men have already died!"

Perhaps ten of the guests heard him. Six of them pushed their chairs back and stood. Their movement caused a momentary lull, and Nick tried again.

"I'm Nicholas Sayre," he said, pointing at his burnt hair and blackened dress shirt, and his bloodied cuffs. "The Chief Minister's nephew. I am not playing games for Dorrance. Look at me, will you! Get out now or you will die here!"

He jumped down as merry pandemonium turned into panic, and almost knocked down the butler who had been standing by either to assist or restrain him, Nick couldn't be sure.

"You're D13, right?" he asked the imposing figure. "There's been an accident downstairs. There is a fire, but there's an... animal loose. Like a tiger, but much stronger, fiercer. No door can hold it. We need to get everyone out on the home meadow, and get them building a ring of hay. Make it about fifty feet in diameter, and we'll gather in the middle and set it alight to keep the animal out. You understand?"

"I believe I do, sir," said the butler with a low bow and a slight glance at Ripton, who nodded. He then turned to look at the footmen who stood impassively against the wall as guests ran past them, some of the latter screaming, some giggling, but most fearful and silent. He tuned his voice to a penetrating pitch and said, "James, Erik, Lancel, Benjamin! You will lead the guests to the home meadow. Lukas, Ned, Luther, Zekall! You will alert Mrs Krane, Mr Rowntree, Mr Gowing and Miss Grayne, to have all their staff immediately go to the home meadow. You will accompany them. Patrick, go and ring the dinner gong for the next three minutes without stopping, then run to the home meadow."

"Good!" snapped Nick. "Don't let anyone stay behind, and if you can take any bottles of paraffin or white spirits out to the meadow, do so! Ripton, lead the way to the library."

"No, sir," said Ripton. "My job's to get you out of here. Come on!"

"We can bar the doors! What the—"

Nick felt himself suddenly restrained by a bearhug around his arms and chest. He tried to throw himself forward, but couldn't move whoever had picked him up. He kicked back, but was held off the ground, his feet uselessly pounding the air.

"Sorry, sir," said Ripton, edging well back so he couldn't be kicked either. "Orders. Take him out to the meadow, Llew."

Nick snapped his head back, hoping to strike his captor's nose, but whoever held him was not only extremely big and strong, but also a practised wrestler. Nick craned around and saw he was in the grip of a very tall and broad footman, one he had noticed when he first arrived, polishing a suit of armour in the entrance hall that, though man-sized, only came up to his shoulder.

"Nay, you shan't escape my clutch, master," said Llew, striding out of the dining room like a determined child with a doll. "Won the belt at Applethwick Fair seven times for the wrestling, I have. You get comfortable and rest. It baint far to the home meadow."

Nick pretended to relax as they joined the column of people going through the main doors and out across the gravelled drive and lawn. It was still quite light, and a harvest moon was rising, big and kind and golden. Many of the people slowed down as the sudden hysteria of Nick's warning ebbed. It was a beautiful night, and the home meadow looked rustic and inviting, with the haycocks still standing, the work of spreading the hay into a defensive ring not yet begun, though the butler was already directing servants to the task.

Halfway across the lawn, Nick suddenly arched his back and tried to twist sideways and out of Llew's grip, but to no avail. The big man just laughed.

The lawn and the meadow were separated by a fence in a ditch, or ha-ha, so as not to spoil the view. Most of the guests and staff were crossing this on a narrow mathematical bridge that featured no nails or screws, but Llew simply climbed down. They were halfway up the other side when there was a sudden, awful screech behind them, a shrill howl that came from no human throat or any animal the Ancelstierrans had ever heard.

"Let me go!" ordered Nick. He couldn't see what was happening, save that the people in front had suddenly started running, many of them off in random directions, not to what he hoped would be safety – if they could get the hay spread quickly enough and get it alight.

"Too late to go back now, sir," said Ripton. "Let him go, Llew! Run!"

Nick looked over his shoulder for a second as they ran the last hundred yards to the centre of the meadow. Smoke was pouring out of one wing of the house, forming a thick, puffy worm that reached up to the sky, black and horrid, with red light flickering at its base. But that was not what held his attention.

The creature was standing on the steps of the house, its head bent over a human victim it carelessly held under one arm. Even from a distance, Nick knew it was drinking blood.

There were people running behind Nick, but not many, and while they might have been tardy seconds before, they were sprinting now. For a moment Nick hoped that nearly everyone had got out of the house. Then he saw movement behind the creature. A man casually walked out to stand next to it. The creature turned to him, and Nick felt the grip of horror as he expected to see it snatch the person up. But it didn't. The creature returned to its first victim and the man stood by its side.

• "Dorrance," said Ripton. He drew his revolver, rested the barrel on his left forearm and aimed for a moment, before holstering the weapon again. "Too far. I'll wait till the bastard's closer."

"Don't worry about Dorrance for the moment," said Nick. He looked around. The guests were all clustered together in the centre of the notional fifty-yard diameter circle, and only the servants were spreading hay, under the direction of the butler. Nick shook his head and walked over to the guests. They surged towards him in turn, once again all speaking at the same time.

"I demand to know—"

"What is going on?"

"Is that... that animal really—"

"Clearly this is not properly—"

"This is an outrage! Who is respons—"

"Shut up!" roared Nick. "Shut up! That animal is from the Old Kingdom! It will kill all of us if we don't keep it out with fire, which is why everybody needs to start spreading hay in the ring! Hurry!"

Without waiting to see their response, Nick ran to the nearest haycock, tore off a huge armful of hay and ran to add it to the circle. When he looked up, some of the guests were helping the servants, but most were still bickering and complaining.

He looked across at the house. The creature was no longer on the steps. There was a body sprawled there, but Dorrance had vanished as well.

"Start pouring the paraffin!" shouted Nick. "Get more hay on the ring! It's coming!"

The butler and some of the footmen began to run around the circle, spraying white petroleum spirit out of four gallon tins.

"Anyone with matches or a cigarette lighter stand by the ring!" yelled Nick. He couldn't see the creature, but his forehead was starting to throb, and when he pulled his dagger out an inch, the Charter marks were beginning to glow.

Two people suddenly jumped the hay and ran across the meadow, heading for the drive and the front gate. A young man and woman, the woman throwing aside her shoes as she ran. It was the one who had come to his door, Nick saw. Tesrya, as she had called herself.

"Come back!" shouted Nick. "Come back—"

His voice fell away as a tall, strange shape emerged from the sunken ditch of the ha-ha, its moonshadow slinking ahead. Its arms looked impossibly long in the twilight, and its legs had three joints, not two. It began to lope slowly after the running couple, and for a brief instant Nick thought perhaps they might have a chance.

Then the creature lowered its head. Its legs stretched, the lope became a run and then a blurring sprint that caught it up with the man and woman in a matter of seconds. It knocked them down with its clubbed hands as it overshot, turning to come back slowly as they flopped about on the ground like fresh-caught fish.

Tesrya was screaming, but the screams stopped abruptly as the creature bent over her.

Nick looked away, and saw a patch of tall yellow flowers near his feet. Corn daisies, fooled into opening by the bright moonlight.

...wrapped in three chains... one of silver, one of lead and one made from braided daisies...

"Ripton!"

"Yes, sir!"

Nick jumped as Ripton answered from slightly behind him and to his left.

"Get anyone who can make flower-chains braiding these daisies, and those poppies over there too. The maids might know how."

"What?"

"I know what it sounds like, but there's a chance that thing can be restrained with chains made from flowers."

"But..."

"The Old Kingdom. Magic. Just make the chains!"

"I knows the braiding of flowers," said Llew, bending down to gently pick a daisy in his huge hand. "As does my kin here, my nieces Ellyn and Alys, who are chambermaids."

"Get to it then, please," said Nick. He looked across at where the young couple had fallen. The creature had been there only seconds ago, but now it was gone. "Damn! Anyone see where it went?"

"No," snapped Ripton. He spun around on the spot as he tried to scan the whole area outside the defensive circle.

"Light the hay! Light the hay! Quickly!"

Ripton struggled with his matches again, striking them on his heel, but others were quicker. Guests with platinum and gold cigarette lighters flicked them open and on and held them to the hay; kitchen staff struck long, heavy-headed matches and threw them; and one old buffer wound and released a clockwork cigar firestarter, an affectation that had finally come into its own.

Accelerated by paraffin, brandy and table polish, the

ring of hay burst into flame. But not everywhere. While the fire leapt high and smoke coiled towards the moon over most of the ring, one segment about ten feet long remained stubbornly dark, dank and unlit. The meadow was sunken there, and wet, and the paraffin had not been spread evenly, pooling in a hole.

"There it is!"

The creature came out of the shadow of the oaks near the drive. Its strangely jointed legs propelled it across the meadow in a sprint that would have let it run down a leopard. It moved impossibly, horribly fast, coming around the outside of the ring. Nick and Ripton started to run too, even though they knew they had no chance of beating the creature.

It would be at the gap in seconds. Only one person was close enough to do anything. A kitchen maid running with a lit taper clutched in her right hand, her left holding up her apron.

The creature was far faster, but it had further to go. It accelerated again, becoming a blur of movement.

Everyone within the ring watched the race, all of them desperately hoping that the fire would simply spread of its own accord, all of them wishing that this fatal hole in their shield of fire would not depend upon a young woman, an easily extinguished taper, and an apron that was too long for its wearer.

Six feet from the edge of the hay, the apron slipped just enough for the girl to trip over the hem. She staggered, tried to recover her balance, and fell, the taper dropping from her hand.

Though she must have been shocked and bruised by the fall, the maid did not lie there. Even as the creature bunched its muscles for the last dash to the gap, the young woman picked up the still-burning taper and threw it the last few feet into the centre of the dark section.

It caught instantly, fed by a pool of paraffin that had collected in the dip in the ground. Blue fire flashed over the hay and flames licked up towards the yellow moon.

The creature shrieked in frustration, its hooked heels throwing up great clods of grass and soil as it checked its headlong rush. For a moment it looked like it might try and jump the fire, but instead it turned and loped back to the ha-ha, disappearing out of sight.

Nick and Ripton stopped and bent over double, resting their hands on their knees, panting as they tried to recover from their desperate sprint.

"It doesn't like fire," coughed out Ripton after a minute. "But we haven't got enough straw to keep this circle going for more than an hour or so. What happens then?"

"I don't know," said Nick. He was acutely aware of his ignorance. None of this would be happening if the creature hadn't drunk his blood. *His* blood, pumping furiously around his body that very second, but a mystery to him. He knew nothing about its peculiar properties. He didn't even know what it could do, or why it had been so strong the creature needed to dilute it with the blood of others.

"Can you do any of that Old Kingdom magic the scouts talk about?"

"No", said Nick. "I... I'm rather useless I'm afraid. I've been planning to go to the Old Kingdom... to learn about, well, a lot of things. But I haven't managed to get there yet."

"So we're pretty well stuffed", said Ripton. "When the fire burns down, that thing will just waltz in here and kill us all."

"We might get help", said Nick.

Ripton snorted. "Not the help we need. I told you. Bullets don't hurt it. I doubt even an artillery shell would do anything, even if a gunner could hit something moving that fast."

"Keep your voice down", muttered Nick. Most of the people inside the ring were huddled right in the centre, as much to get away from the drifting smoke of the fires as for the psychological ease of being further away from the creature. But a knot of half a dozen guests and servants were only a dozen yards away, the servants helping up the kitchen maid and the guests getting in the way. "I meant Old Kingdom help. I sent a message with Malthan. A telegram for him to send to some people who can get a message to the Old Kingdom quickly."

Ripton bent his head and mumbled something.

"What? What did you say?"

"Malthan never made it past the village", Ripton muttered. "I handed him over to two of Hodgeman's particular pals at the crossroads. Orders. I had to do it, to maintain my cover."

Nick was silent, his thoughts on the sad, frightened, greedy little man who was now probably dead in a ditch not too many miles away.

"Hodgeman said you'd never follow up what happened to Malthan," said Ripton. "He said your sort never did. You were just throwing your weight around, he said."

"I would have checked," said Nick. "I would have left no stone unturned. Believe me."

He looked around at the ring of fire. Sections of it were already dying down, generating lots of smoke but little flame. If Malthan had managed to send the telegram six or more hours ago, there might have been a slim chance that the Abhorsen... or Lirael... or somebody competent to deal with the creature would have been able to get there before they ran out of things to burn.

"Hodgeman's dead now, anyway. He was one of the first that thing got."

"I sent another message," said Nick. "I bribed Danjer's valet to go down to the village and send a telegram."

"Nowhere to send one from there," said Ripton. "Planned that way, of course. D13 keeping control of communications. The closest telephone would be at Colonel Wrale's house, and that's ten miles away."

"I don't suppose he would have managed it anyway..."

Nick broke off and peered at the closer group of people and then at the central muddle, wiping his eyes as a tendril of smoke wafted across.

"Where is Danjers? I don't remember seeing him at the dinner table, and he's pretty hard to miss. What's the butler's name again?"

"Whitecrake," said Ripton, but Nick was already striding across to the butler, who was issuing orders to his footmen, who were busy feeding the fires with more straw.

"Whitecrake!" Nick called before he had half-covered the thirty yards between them. "Where is Mr Danjers?"

Whitecrake rotated with great dignity, rather like a dreadnaught's gun turret, and bowed, allowing Nick to close the distance before he replied.

"Mr Danjers removed himself from the party and left at five o'clock," he said. "I understand that the curtains in the dining room clashed with his waistcoat."

"His man went with him?"

"Naturally," said Whitecrake. "I believe Mr Danjers intended motoring over to Applethwick."

Nick felt every muscle in his shoulders and neck suddenly relax, as a ripple of relief passed through on its way to his toes.

"We'll be all right! Danjer's valet is bound to send that telegram! Let's see, if they got to Applethwick by seven-thirty... the telegram would be at Wyverley by eight at the latest... they'd get the message on to the Abhorsen's House however they do it... then if someone flew by Paperwing to Wyverley, they've got those aeroplanes at the flying school there to fly south... though I suppose not at night, even with this moon..."

The tension started to come back as Nick came to the realisation that even if the Abhorsen or King Touchstone's Guard had already received his message, there was no way anyone could be at Dorrance Hall before the morning, at the very earliest.

Nick looked up from the fingers he'd been counting on and saw that Ripton, Whitecrake, several footmen, a couple of maids and a number of the guests were all hanging on his every word.

"Help will be coming," Nick announced firmly. "But we have to make the fires last as long as we can. Everything that can burn must be gathered within this ring. Every tiny piece of straw, any spare clothes, papers you may have on you, even banknotes... need to be gathered up. Mr Whitecrake, can you take charge of that? Ripton, a word if you don't mind."

No one objected to Nick taking command and he hardly noticed himself that he had. He had often taken the lead among his schoolfriends and at university, his mind usually grasping any situation faster than his fellows, and his aristocratic heritage providing more than enough self-belief. As he turned away and walked closer to the fire, Ripton followed at his heels like an obedient shadow.

"There won't be any useful help till morning at the earliest," Nick whispered, his voice hardly audible over the crackle of the fire. "I mean Old Kingdom help. Provided Danjer's man did send the telegram."

Ripton eyed the burning straw.

"I suppose there's a chance the fire'll last till dawn, if we rake it narrower and just try to maintain a bit of flame and coals. Do you... is there a possibility that... that thing doesn't like the sun, as well as fire?"

"I don't know. But I wouldn't count on it. From the little I heard my friend Sam talk about it at school, these kind of Free Magic creatures roam the day as freely as they do the night."

"Maybe it'll run out of puff," said Ripton. "Like you said. Dorrance didn't expect it to even wake up, and here it is running around—"

"What's that noise?" interrupted Nick. He could hear a distant jangling noise, carried on the light breeze towards him. "Is that a bell?"

"Oh no... " groaned Ripton. "It's the volunteer fire brigade from the village. They know they're not to come here, no matter what—"

Nick looked around at the ring of red fire, and beyond that, the vast column of spark-lit smoke that was winding up from Dorrance Hall. No firefighter would be able to resist that clarion call.

"They're probably only the first," he said quietly. "With this moon, the smoke will be visible for miles. We'll probably have town brigades here in an hour or so, as well as all the local volunteers for a dozen miles or more. I'll have to stop them."

"What! If you leave the ring that monster will be on you in a second!"

Nick shook his head.

"I've been thinking about that. It ran away from me after it drank just a little of my blood. Dorrance was yelling something about getting it other blood to dilute mine. It could easily have killed me then, but it didn't."

"You can't go out," said Ripton. "Think about it! It's drunk enough in the last hour to dilute your blood a hundred times over! It could easily be ready for more. And it's *your* blood that revved it up in the first place. It'll kill you and get more powerful, and then it'll kill us!"

"We can't just let it kill the firemen," said Nick stubbornly. He started to walk to the other side of the circle, closer to the drive. Ripton hurried along beside him. "I might be able to hurt... even kill... the creature with this."

He pulled out Sam's dagger and held it up. Fire and moonlight reflected from the blade, but there was green and blue and gold there too as Charter marks swam slowly across the metal. Not fully active, but still strange and wonderful under the Ancelstierran moon.

Ripton did not seem overly impressed.

"You'd never got close enough to use that little pigsticker. Llew! Llew!"

"You're not catching me like that again," said Nick, without slowing down. He stowed the dagger away and picked up a rake, ready to make a gap in the burning barrier. A glance over his shoulder showed him the huge-shouldered Llew getting up from where he was braiding flowers. "If I want to go, you're going to let me this time."

"Too late," said Ripton. "There's the fire engine."

He pointed through the smoke. An ancient, horse-drawn tanker of a kind obsolete everywhere, save the most rural counties, was coming up the drive, with at least fourteen volunteer firemen crammed on or hanging off it. They were in various states of uniform, but all wore gleaming brass helmets. Several other firemen on horseback came behind the engine, followed by a farm truck, loaded with more irregular volunteers armed with firebeaters and buckets. Two small cars brought up the rear, transporting another four brass-helmeted volunteers.

"How did they—"

"There's another entrance to the estate by the gamekeeper's cottage, cuts half a mile off the front drive."

Nick plunged at the fire with the rake and dragged some of the burning hay aside before he had to fall back from the smoke and heat. After a few seconds to recover, he pushed forward again, widening the gap. But it was going to take a few minutes to get through, and the firemen would be at the meadow before he could get out.

After Nick's third attempt he reeled back into the grasp of Llew, who held him as he tried to swipe his legs with the rake, till Ripton grabbed it and twisted it out of his hands.

"Hold hard, master!" said Llew.

"It's not attacking them!" cried Ripton. "Just keep still and take a look."

74

Nick stopped struggling. The fire engine had come to a halt as close as the men and horses could stand the heat, some fifty yards from the house. Firemen leapt off on to the lawn and began to bustle about with hoses, as the truck and cars screeched to a halt behind them, throwing up gravel. The two mounted firemen continued on towards the meadow, their horses' hooves clattering on the narrow bridge over the ha-ha.

"It'll take the horsemen," said Nick. "It *must* be hiding in the ditch."

But the riders passed unmolested over the bridge and across the meadow, finally wheeling about close enough to the ring of fire for one of them to shout:

"What on earth is happening here?"

Nick didn't bother to answer. He was still looking for the creature. Why hadn't it attacked?

Then he saw it, through the swirling smoke. Not attacking anyone, but slinking up from the ha-ha and across the meadow towards the drive. Dorrance was riding on its back, like a child on a bizarre mobile toy, his arms clasped around the creature's long neck. He pointed towards the gatehouse and the creature began to run.

"It's running away!" exclaimed Ripton.

"It's running," said Nick. "I wonder where?"

"Who cares!" exclaimed Ripton happily.

"I do," said Nick. He slipped free of the suddenly relaxed grasp of Llew and Ripton, took a deep, relatively smoke-free breath, sprinted forward and jumped the ring of fire where he'd already partially made a gap.

He landed clear, fell forward and quickly rolled in the grass to extinguish any flames that might have hitched a ride. He felt hot, but not burnt, and he had not breathed in any great concentration of smoke.

Looking back he saw Ripton and Llew frantically raking the fire apart, but they had not dared to jump after him. He got up and ran towards the lawn, the parked cars, the fire engine and the burning house.

There was only one reason the creature would flee now. It had nothing to fear from any weapons the Ancelstierrans could bring to bear. It could have stayed and killed everybody and drunk their blood. It must have decided to cut and run because the power it had gained from Nick's blood was waning and it didn't dare drink any more from him. That meant it would be heading north, towards the Old Kingdom, to find fresh victims to replenish its strength. Victims who bore the Charter mark on their foreheads.

Nick couldn't let it do that.

He reached the rearmost car and vaulted into the driver's seat, deaf to the roar of the fire, the thud of the pumps and the contained shriek of the high-pressure hoses. Even when Nick pressed the starter button, none of the firemen looked around, the sound of the little two-seater's engine lost amid all the noise and action.

The car was a Branston Four convertible, very similar to the Branston roadster Nick used to hire occasionally when he was at Sunbere. He slapped the gear lever with the necessary double-tap into reverse and gently pulled the hand throttle. The little car rolled back on to the lawn. Nick tapped the lever into the first of the two forward gears and nudged forward.

The firemen still hadn't noticed, but as Nick opened the hand throttle up, the car backfired, hopped forward and stalled. Someone, presumably the owner of the car, shouted something. Nick saw a bronze-helmeted head approaching in the wing mirror. To his left, Ripton and Llew charged up out of the ha-ha.

He depressed the clutch, hit the starter again, and hoped he had the throttle position right. The car backfired again, leapt six feet forward, and then the engine suddenly hit a sweet, drumming note. The speedometer stopped hiccupping up and down and steadily rose towards the top speed of thirty-five miles per hour. A breeze ruffled Nick's hair, undiminished by the tiny windshield.

The bronze helmet disappeared from the mirror as the car accelerated along the drive. Ripton and Llew got almost close enough to lay a hand on the rear bumper, before they too were left behind. Ripton shouted something and, a second later, Nick felt something rebound off his shoulder and land on the seat next to him.

He glanced down and saw a chain of yellow daisies, punctuated every ten blooms or so with a red poppy.

Nick didn't bother switching on the car's headlights. The moon was so bright that he could even read the dashboard dials, and he could see the drive clearly. What he couldn't see was the creature and Dorrance, but he had to presume they were heading for the front gate. The wall around the estate was probably no great barrier to the creature, but if it didn't need to climb it, he hoped it wouldn't.

His guess was rewarded as he turned out of the gate, and stopped to look in both directions, up and down the lane. It was darker here, the road shadowed by the trees on either side. But on a slight rise, several hundred yards distant, Nick caught sight of the odd silhouette of the creature, with Dorrance still riding on its back. It disappeared over the crest, running very fast and keeping to the road.

Nick sped after it, the little car vibrating as he wrenched the hand throttle out as far as it would go. The speedometer went past the curlicued '35' and got stuck against the raised letter 'n' that completed the word 'Branston' on the dial. But even at that speed, by the time he got to the top of the rise, the creature and Dorrance were gone. The lane kept on, with a very gentle curve to the left, so if Nick's quarry was anywhere within a mile, he should have been able to see them in the clear, cool light of the vast moon overhead.

Various possibilities whisked through Nick's mind. The most disturbing was the thought that they had seen him, and were hiding off the road, the creature ready to spring on to him as he passed. But the most likely possibility quickly replaced this fear. He hadn't seen it at first, because of the trees, but another road joined the lane just before it started to curve away. The creature must have gone that way.

Nick took the corner a little too fast, the car sliding off the paved road and on to the verge, sending up a spray of clods and loose road-metal. For a moment he felt the back end start to slide out, and the steering wheel was loose in his hands, as if it was no longer connected to anything. Then the tyres bit again, and he over-corrected and fishtailed furiously for thirty yards before getting fully under control.

When he could properly look ahead, Nick couldn't see the creature and Dorrance. But this road only continued for another two hundred yards, ending at a small railway station. It was not much more than a signal box, a rudimentary waiting room, a platform, and the stationmaster's house set some distance away. A single line of track looped in from the southwest, ran along the platform, then looped back out again, to join the main line that ran straight and true a few minute's walk away.

It had to be Dorrance Halt, the private railway station for Dorrance Hall. There was a train waiting at the platform, grey-white smoke busily puffing out of the locomotive and steam wafting around its wheels. A strangely-configured train, because there were six empty flat cars behind the engine, then a private car. Dorrance's private car, with his crest upon the doors.

Nick suddenly realised the significance of the blazon of the silver chain. Dorrance's several-times great grandfather must have been the Captain Inquirer who found the creature, and the money gained from the sale of a silver chain only part of the current Dorrance's inheritance.

The significance of the empty flat cars was also apparent to Nick. They were there to separate the locomotive from any Free Magic interference caused by the creature. Dorrance had thought out this mode of transport very carefully. Perhaps he had always planned to take the creature away by train. The thing's long-term goal must always have been to return to the Old Kingdom.

Even as Nick pushed the little Branston to its utmost, the locomotive whistled and began to pull out of the station. As the rearmost carriage passed the waiting room, the electric lights outside fizzed and exploded. The train slowly picked up speed, the gouts of smoke from its funnel coming faster as it rolled away.

Nick wrenched the throttle completely out of its housing, drove off the road, raced through the station garden in a cloud of broken stakes and tomato plants, and drove on to the platform in a desperate effort to crash into the train and stop the creature's escape.

But he was too late. All he could do was lock his knee and try and push his foot and the brake pedal through the floor, as the Branston squealed and slid down the platform, only prevented from sliding off the end by a slow-speed impact with a large and very sturdy line of flowerpots.

Nick stood up and watched the train rattle on to the main line. For a moment, he thought he saw the glow of the creature's violet eyes looking back at him through the rear window of the carriage. But, he told himself as he put the flower chain around his neck and then jumped out of the badly-dented Branston, it was probably just a reflection from the moon.

A sound from the waiting room made Nick jump and draw his dagger, but he sheathed it again straight away. A man wearing a railway uniform coat over blue-striped pyjamas was standing in the doorway, staring as Nick had just done, after the departing train.

"Where's that train going?" demanded Nick. "When's the next train here?"

"I... I... saw a real monster!" said the man. His eyes were wide with what Nick at first thought was shock, but slowly realised was actually delight. "I saw a monster!"

"You're lucky it left you alive to remember it," said Nick. "Now answer my questions! You're the stationmaster, aren't you? Get a grip on yourself!"

The man nodded, but didn't look at Nick. He kept staring after the train, even as it disappeared from sight.

"Where's that train going?"

"I... I don't know. It's Mr Dorrance's private train. It's been waiting for days, the crew sleeping over at the house... then the call came only an hour ago, to be ready. It got a slot going north, that's all I know, direct from Central at Corvere. I guess it'd be going to Bain. You know, I never thought I'd see something like that, with those huge eyes, and those spiked hands. Not here, not—"

"When's the next train north?"

"*The Bain Flyer*," the man replied automatically. "But she's an express. She doesn't stop anywhere, least of all here."

"When is it due to go past?"

"Ten oh five."

Nick looked at the clock above the waiting room, but like the electric light, it had ceased to function. There was a watch-chain hanging out of the stationmaster's pocket, so he snagged that and drew out a regulation railway watch. Clockwork did not suffer so much from Free Magic, and its second hand was cheerfully moving round. According to the watch, it was three minutes to ten.

"What's the signal for an obstruction on the line?" snapped Nick.

"Three flares, two outside, one in the track," said the man. He suddenly looked at Nick, his attention returned to the here and now. "But you're not—"

"Where are the flares?"

The stationmaster shook his head, but couldn't hide an instinctive glance towards a large red box on the wall to the left of the ticket window.

"Don't try to stop me," said Nick very forcefully. "Go back to your house and, if your phone's working, call the police. Tell them... Oh, there's no time! Tell them whatever you like."

The flares were ancient, foot-long things like batons, that came in two parts which had to be screwed together to mix the chemicals that in turn ignited the magnesium core. Nick grabbed a handful and rushed over the branch line to the main track. Or what he hoped was the main track. There were four railway lines next to each other and he couldn't be absolutely sure which one Dorrance's train had taken heading north.

Even if he got it wrong, he told himself, any driver seeing three red flares close would almost certainly stop. He quickly screwed the first flare together and dropped it in the track, then the other two followed quickly, one to either side.

With the flares gushing bright blue magnesium and red iron flames, Nick decided he couldn't afford explanations, so he crossed the tracks and crouched down behind a tree to wait.

He didn't have to wait long. He had barely looked over his shoulder at the expanding pall of smoke that now covered a good quarter of the sky before he heard the distant sound of a fast-moving, big train. Then, only seconds after the noise, he saw the triple headlights of the engine as it raced down the track towards him. A moment later, there was the shriek of the whistle, and then the awful screech of metal on metal as the driver applied the brakes, a screech that intensified every few seconds as the emergency brakes in each of the following carriages came on hard as well.

Nick, hearing the horrid scream of emergency-braking and seeing the sheer speed of the approaching lights, suddenly remembered the boast of the North-by-Northwest Railway, that its trains averaged 110 miles per hour, and for a fearful moment he wondered if he'd made a terrible mistake. It was one thing to risk his life pursuing the creature. Quite another if he was responsible for derailing *The Bain Flyer* and killing all the passengers on board.

But despite the noise and speed, the train was slowing under total control on a long straight. It came to a shrieking, sparking halt just short of the flares.

Even before it completely stopped, a driver jumped down from the engine, and conductors leapt from almost every one of the fifteen carriages. No one got out on the far side, so it was relatively easy for Nick to run from his tree, climb the steps of a second-class carriage and go inside. Without being observed, or so he hoped.

The carriage was split into compartments, with a passageway running down the side. Nick quickly glanced in the first compartment. It had six passengers in it, almost the full complement of eight. Most of them were squashed together trying to look out the window, though one was asleep and another reading the paper with studied detachment. For a brief second, Nick thought of going in, but he dismissed the notion immediately. The passengers would have been together for hours, and the appearance of a bloodied, blackened young man with burnt eyebrows could not go unnoticed or unremarked. Somehow, Nick doubted that any explanation he could provide would satisfy the passengers, let alone the conductor.

Instead, Nick looked up at the luggage rack that ran the length of the carriage. It was pretty full, but he saw a less-populated section. Even as he hoisted himself up and discovered that his chosen resting place was on top of a set of golf-clubs and an umbrella, the engine whistled twice, followed by the sound of doors slamming, and then the appearance of a conductor and two large, annoyed male passengers, who had just come back aboard.

"I don't know what the railway's coming to."

"Rack and ruin, that's what."

"Now, now, gentlemen, no harm's done. We'll make up our time, you'll see. We're expected in at twenty-five minutes after midnight, and *The Bain Flyer* is never late. The railway will buy you a drink or two at the station hotel, and all will be right with the world."

If only that were so, thought Nicholas Sayre. He waited for the men to move along, then wriggled into a slightly less uncomfortable position and rearranged the flower chain across his chest so it would not get crumpled. He lay there, thinking about what had happened and what could happen, and built up plan after plan, like he used to build matchstick towers as a boy, only to have them suffer the same fate. At some point, they always fell over.

Finally, it hit him. Dorrance and the creature had got away. At least, they'd got away from him. His part in the whole sorry disaster was over. Even if Dorrance's special train was going to Bain, they would arrive at least half an hour ahead of Nick. And there was a good chance that Ripton would have made it to a phone, so the authorities would be alerted. The police in Bain had some experience with things crossing the Wall from the Old Kingdom. They'd get help, Charter Mages from the Crossing Point Scouts. There would be lots of people much more qualified than Nick to deal with the creature.

At least I tried, Nick thought. *When I see Lirael... and Nick... and the Abhorsen, though I hope I don't have to explain it to her, then I can honestly say I really did my best. I mean, even if I had managed to catch up with them, I don't know if I'd have been able to do anything. Maybe my Charter-spelled dagger would have worked... maybe I could have tried something else...*

Nick suddenly felt very tired, and sore, the weariness more urgent than the pain. Even his feet hurt, and for the first time he realised he was still wearing carpet slippers. He was sure his shoes had been wonderfully shined, but by now they would be ash in the ruins of Dorrance Hall.

Nick shook his head at the thought, pushed back on the golf bag and without meaning to, fell instantly asleep.

He woke to find something gripping his elbow. Instantly he lashed out with his fist, connecting with something fleshy rather than the scaly, hard surface his dreaming mind had suggested might be the case.

"Ow!"

A young man dressed in ludicrously bright golfing tweeds looked up at Nick, his hand covering his nose. Other passengers were already in the corridor, most of them with their bags in hand already. The train had arrived in Bain.

"You've broken my dose!"

"Sorry!" said Nick, as he vaulted down. "I'm very sorry! Mistaken identity. Thought you were a monster."

"I say!" called out the man. "Wait a moment. You can't just hit a man and run away!"

"Urgent business!" Nick replied as he ran to the door, weaving past several other passengers, who quickly stood aside. "Nicholas Sayre's the name. Many apologies!"

He jumped out on to the platform, half-expecting to see it swarming with police, soldiers and ambulance attendants. He would be able to report to someone in authority and then check in to the hotel for a proper rest.

But there was only the usual bustle of a big country station in the middle of the night, with the last important train finally in. Passengers were disembarking. Porters were gathering cases. A newspaper vendor was hawking a late edition of the *Times*, shouting, "Flood kills five men, three horses. Getcher paper! Flood kills three—"

There'd be a different headline in the next edition, Nick thought, though it almost certainly wouldn't be the real story. 'Fire at country house' would be most likely, with the survivors paid or pressured to shut up. He would probably get to read it over breakfast, which reminded him that he was extremely hungry and needed to have a very late, much-delayed dinner. Of course, in order to eat, he'd need to get some money, and that meant...

"Excuse me, sir, could I see your ticket please?"

Nick's train of thought derailed spectacularly. A railway inspector was standing too close to him, looking sternly at the dishevelled, blackened, eyebrow-less young man in ruined evening wear with a chain of braided daisies around his neck and carpet slippers on his feet.

"Ah, good evening," replied Nick. He patted his sides and tried to look somewhat tipsy and confused, which was not hard. "I'm afraid I seem to have lost my ticket. And my coat. And for that matter, my tie. But if I could make a telephone call I'm sure everything can be put right."

"Undergraduate are you sir?" asked the inspector. "Put on the train by your friends?"

"Something like that," admitted Nick.

"I'll have your name and college to start with," said the inspector stolidly. "Then we can see about a telephone call."

"Nicholas Sayre," replied Nick. "Sunbere. Though technically I'm not up this term."

"Sayre?" asked the inspector. "Would you be—"

"My uncle, I'm afraid," said Nick. "That's who I need to call. At the Golden Sheaf Hotel, near Applethwick. I'm sure that if there is a fine to pay I'll be able to sort something out."

"You'll just have to purchase a ticket before you leave the station," said the inspector. "As for the phone call, follow me and you can—"

He stopped talking as Nick suddenly turned away from him and stared up at the pedestrian bridge that crossed the railway tracks. To the right, the direction of the station hotel and most of the town, everything was normal, the bridge crowded with passengers off the *Flyer* eager to get to the hotel or home. But to the lonely left, the electric lights on the wrought iron lampposts were flickering and going out. One after the other, each one died just as two porters passed by, wheeling a very long, tall box.

"It must be the— But Dorrance was half an hour ahead of the *Flyer*!"

"You're involved in one of Mr Dorrance's japes, are you?" smiled the inspector. "His train just came in, on the old track. Private trains aren't allowed on the express line. Hey! Sir! Come back!"

Nick ran, vaulting the ticket inspection barrier, the inspector's shouts ignored behind him. All of his resignation burnt away in an instant. The creature was here, and he was still the only one who knew about it.

Two policemen belatedly moved to intercept him before the stairs, but they were too slow. Nick jumped up the steps three at a time. He almost fell at the top step, but turned the movement into a fleche to launch himself into a sprint across the bridge.

At the top of the stairs at the other end, he slowed and drew his dagger. Down below, at the side of the road, the tall box was lying on its side, open. One of the two porters was sprawled next to it, his throat ripped out.

There was a row of shops on the other side of the street, all shuttered and dark. The single lamppost was also dark. The moon was lower now, and the shadows deeper. Nick walked down the steps, dagger ready, the Charter marks swimming on the blade bright enough to shed light. He could hear police whistles behind him, and knew that they would be there in moments, but he spared no attention from the street.

Nothing moved there, until Nick left the last step. As he trod on the road, the creature suddenly emerged from an alcove between two shops, and dropped the second porter at its hoofed feet. Its violet eyes shone with a deep, internal fire now, and its black teeth were rimmed with red flames. It made a sound that was half-hiss and half-growl, and raised its spiked club hands. Nick tensed for its attack and tried to fumble the flower-chain off his neck with his left hand.

Then Dorrance peered over the creature's shoulder and whispered something in its ear-slit. The thing blinked, single eyelids sliding across to dim rather than close its burning violet eyes. Then it suddenly jumped more than twenty feet — but away from Nick. Dorrance, clinging on for dear life, shouted as it sped away.

"Stay back, Sayre! It just wants to go home."

Nick started to run, but stopped after only a dozen strides, the creature disappearing into the dark. It had evidently not exhausted all the power it had gained from Nick's blood, or perhaps simply being closer to the Old Kingdom lent it strength.

Panting, his chest heaving from his exertion, Nick looked back. The two policemen were coming down the stairs, their truncheons in hand. The fact that they were still approaching indicated they had not seen the creature.

Nick sheathed his dagger and held up his hands. The policemen slowed to a walk and approached warily. Then Nick saw a single headlight approaching rapidly towards him. A motorcycle. He stepped out into the street and waved his hand furiously to flag the rider down.

The motorcyclist stopped next to Nick. He was young and sported a small, highly-trimmed moustache that did him no favours.

"What occurs, old man?"

"No time to explain," gasped Nick. "I need your bike. Name's Sayre. Nicholas."

"The fast bowler!" exclaimed the rider as he casually stepped off the idling bike, holding it upright for Nick to get on. He was unperturbed by the sight of Nick's strange attire or the shouts of the policemen who had starting to run again. "I saw you play here last year. Wonderful match! There you are. Bring the old girl back to Wooten, if you don't mind. St John Wooten, in Bain."

"Pleasure!" said Nick as he pushed off and kicked the motorcycle into gear. It rattled away, barely ahead of the running policemen, one of whom threw his truncheon, striking Nick a glancing blow on the shoulder.

"Good shot!" cried St John Wooten, but the policemen were soon left behind as easily as the creature had left Nick.

For a few minutes, Nick thought he might catch up with his quarry fairly soon. The motorcycle was new and powerful, a far cry from the school gardener's old Vernal Victrix he'd learned on back at Somersby. But after almost sliding out on several corners and getting the wobbles at speed, Nick had to acknowledge that his lack of experience was the limiting factor, not the machine's capacity. He slowed down to a point just slightly beyond his competence, a speed insufficient to do more than occasionally catch a glimpse of the creature and Dorrance ahead.

As Nick expected, they soon left even the outskirts of Bain behind, turning right on to the Bain High Road. Heading north. There was very little traffic on the road, and what there was of it was heading the other way. At least until the creature ran past. Those cars or trucks that didn't run off the road as the driver saw the monster stalled to a stop, their electrics destroyed by the creature's passage. Nick, coming up only a minute or so later, never even saw the drivers. As might be expected this far north, they had instantly fled the scene, looking for running water or, at the very least, some friendly walls.

The question of what the creature would do at the first Perimeter checkpoint was easily answered. When Nick saw the warning sign he slowed, not wanting to be shot. But when he idled up to the red-striped barrier, there were four dead soldiers lying in a row, their heads caved in. The creature had killed them without even slowing down. None of the soldiers had managed to get a shot off, though the officer had his revolver in his hand. They hadn't been wearing mail this far south, or the characteristic neck- and nasal-barred helmets of the Perimeter garrison. After all, trouble came from the north. This most southern checkpoint was the relatively friendly face of the Army, there to turn back unauthorised travellers or tourists.

Nick was about to go straight on, but he knew there were more stringent checkpoints ahead, before the Perimeter proper, and the chance of being shot would greatly increase. So he put the motorcycle in neutral, sat it on its stand and, looking away as much as he could, took the cleanest tunic, which happened to be the officer's. It had a second lieutenant's single pip on each cuff. The previous wearer had probably been much the same age as Nick, and moments before must have been proud of his small command, before he lost it, with his life.

Nick figured wearing the khaki coat would at least give him time to explain who he was before he was shot at. He shrugged it on, left it unbuttoned with the flower-chain underneath, got back on the motorcycle and set off once more.

He heard several shots before he arrived at the next checkpoint, and a brief staccato burst of machine-gun fire, followed a few seconds later by a rocket arcing up into the night. It burst into three red parachute flares that slowly drifted north-norwest, propelled by a southerly wind that would usually give comfort to the soldiers of the Perimeter. They would not have been expecting any trouble.

The second checkpoint was a much more serious affair than the first, blocking the road with two heavy chain-link and timber gates, built between concrete pillboxes that punctuated the first of the Perimeter's many defensive lines, a triple depth of barbed concertina wire five coils high that stretched to the east and west as far as the eye could see.

One of the gates had been knocked off its hinges, and there were more bodies on the ground just beyond it. These soldiers had been wearing mail coats and helmets, but it hadn't saved them. More soldiers were running out of the pillboxes, and there were several in firing positions to the side of the road, though they'd stopped shooting, due to the risk of hitting their own people further north.

Nick throttled back and weaved the motorcycle through the slalom course of bodies, debris from the gate and the live but shaken soldiers who were staring north. He was just about to accelerate away when someone shouted behind him.

"You on the motorcycle! Stop!"

Nick felt an urge to open the throttle and let the motorcycle roar away, but his intelligence overruled his instinct. He stopped and looked back, wincing as the thin sole of his left carpet slipper tore on a piece of broken barbed wire.

The man who had shouted ran up and, greatly surprising Nick, jumped on the pillion seat behind him.

"Get after it!"

Nick only had a moment to gain a snapshot of his sudden passenger. He was an officer, not visibly armed, wearing formal dress blues with more miniatures of gallantry medals than he should have since he looked no more than twenty-one. He had the three pips of a Captain on his sleeve and, most importantly, on his shoulders the metal epaulette tags NPRU, for the Northern Perimeter Reconaissance Unit, or as it was better known, the Crossing Point Scouts.

"I know you, don't I?" shouted the Captain over the noise of the engine and rush of the wind. "You tried out for the Scouts last week?"

"Uh, no," Nick shouted back. He had just realised that he knew his passenger too. It was Francis Tindall, who had been at Forwin Mill as a lieutenant six months ago. "I'm afraid I'm... well, I'm Nicholas Sayre."

"Nick Sayre! I bloody hope this isn't going to be like last time we met!"

"No! But that creature is a Free Magic thing!"

"Got a hostage too, from the look of it. Skinny old duffer. Pointless carrying him along. We'll still shoot."

"He's an accomplice. It's already killed a lot of people down south."

"Don't worry, we'll settle its hash," Tindall shouted confidently. "You don't happen to know exactly what kind of Free Magic creature it is? Can't say I've ever seen anything like it, but I only got a glimpse. Didn't expect anything like that to run past the window at a dining-in night at Checkpoint Two."

"No, but it's bulletproof and it gets power by drinking the blood of Charter Mages."

Whatever Tindall said in response was lost in the sound of gunfire up ahead, this time long repeated bursts of machine-gun fire, and Nick saw red tracer bouncing up into the air.

"Slow down!" ordered Tindall. "Those are the enfilading guns at Lizzy and Pearl. They'll stop firing when the thing hits the gate at Checkpoint One."

Nick obediently slowed. The road was straight ahead of them, but dark, the moon having sunk further. Red tracer was the only thing visible, criss-crossing the road four or five hundred yards ahead of them.

Then big guns boomed in unison.

"Star-shell," said Tindall. "Thanks to a southerly wind."

A second after he spoke, four small suns burst high above and everything became stark black-and-white, either harshly lit or in blackest shadow.

In the light, Nick saw another deep defensive line of high concertina wire, and another set of gates. He also saw the creature slow not at all, but simply jump up twenty feet and over thirty feet of wire, smashing its way past the two or three fast but foolish soldiers who tried to stick a bayonet in it as it hit the ground running.

Dorrance was no longer on its back.

Nick saw him a moment later, lying in the middle of the road. Braking hard, he lost control of the bike at the last moment, and it flipped up and out, throwing both him and Tindall on to the road, but fortunately not at any speed.

Nick lay there for a moment, the breath knocked out of him by the impact. After a minute, he slowly got to his feet. Captain Tindall was already standing, but only on one foot.

"Busted ankle," he said as he hopped over to Dorrance. "Why, it's that idiot jester Dorrance! What on earth would someone like him be doing with that creature?"

"Serving Her," whispered Dorrance, his voice startling both Tindall and Nick. The older man had been shot several times and looked dead, his chest black and sodden with blood. But he opened his eyes and looked directly at Nick, though he clearly saw something or someone else. "I knew Her as a child, in my dreams, never knowing She was real. Then Malthan came, and I saw Her picture, and I remembered Father sending Her away. He was mad, you know. Lackridge found Her for me again. It was as I remembered, Her voice in my head… She only wanted to go home. I had to help Her. I had to…"

His voice trailed away and his eyes lost their focus. Dorrance would play the fool no more in Corvere.

"If it wants to go north, I suppose we could do worse than just let it go across the Wall," said Tindall. He waved at someone at the checkpoint and made a signal, crossing his arms twice. "If it can, of course. We can send a pigeon to the Guards at Barhedrin, leave it to them to sort out."

"No, I can't do that," said Nick. "I… I'm already responsible for loosing the Destroyer upon them, and I did nothing to help fight it. Now I've done it again. That creature would not be free if it wasn't for me. I can't just leave it to Lirael, I mean the Abhorsen… or whoever."

"Some things are best left to those who can deal with them," said Tindall. "I've never seen a Free Magic creature move like that. Let it go."

"No," said Nick. He started walking up the road. Tindall swore and started hopping after him.

"What are you going to do? You have the mark, I know, but are you a mage?"

Nick shook his head and started to run. A sergeant and two stretcher bearers were coming through the gate, while many more soldiers ran purposefully behind them. With star-shell continuing to be fired overhead, Nick could clearly see beyond the gates, to a parade ground, with a viewing tower or inspection platform next to it, and beyond that, a collection of low huts and bunkers and the communication trenches that zigzagged north.

"The word for the day is 'Collection' and the countersign 'Treble'," shouted Tindall. "Good luck!"

Nick waved his thanks and concentrated on ignoring the pain in his feet. Both his slippers were ripped to pieces, barely more than shreds of cloth holding on at the heel and toes.

The sergeant saluted as he went past and the stretcher-bearers ignored him, but the two soldiers at the gate aimed their rifles at him and demanded the password. Nick gave it, silently thanking Tindall, and they let him through.

"Lieutenant! Report!" shouted a major who Nick almost ran into as he entered the communication trench on the northern side of the parade ground. But he ignored the instruction, dodging past the officer. A few steps further on, he felt something warm strike his back, and his arms and hands suddenly shone with golden Charter Magic fire. It didn't harm him at all, but actually made him feel better, and helped him recover his breath. He ran on, oblivious to the shocked Charter Mage behind him, who had struck him with his strongest spell of binding and immobility.

Soldiers stood aside as he ran past, the Charter Magic glow alerting them to his coming. Some cheered in his wake, for they had seen the creature leap over them and they feared that it might return before a Scout came to deal with it, as they dealt with so many of the strange things that came from the north.

At the forward trench, Nick found himself suddenly amongst a whole company of garrison infantry. All hundred and twenty of them clustered close together in less than sixty yards of straight trench, all standing-to on the firing step, looking to the front. The wind was still from the south, so their guns would almost certainly work, but none were firing.

A harried-looking captain turned to see what had caused the sudden ripple of movement among the men near the communication trench, and saw a strange, very irregularly-dressed lieutenant outlined in tiny golden flames. He breathed a sigh of relief, hopped down from the step and stood in front of Nick.

"About time one of you lot got here. It's ploughing through the wire towards the Wall. D Company shot at it for a while, but that didn't work, so we've held back. It's not going to turn around is it?"

"Probably not," said Nick, words which did not offer the certainty the captain had hoped for. He saw a ladder and quickly climbed up it to stand on the parapet.

The Wall lay less than a hundred yards away, across barren earth crisscrossed with wire. There were tall poles of carved wood here and there too, quietly whistling in the breeze, amongst the metal pickets and the concertina wire. Wind flutes of the Abhorsen, there to bar the way from Death. A great many people had died all along the Wall and the Perimeter, and the border between Life and Death was very easily crossed in such places.

Nick had seen the Wall before, farewelling his friend Sam on vacation. But apart from a dream-like memory of it wreathed in fierce golden fire, he had never seen it as more than an antiquity, just an old wall like any other medieval remnant in a state of good preservation. Now he could see the glow of millions of Charter marks moving across, through and under the stones.

He could see the creature too. It was surrounded by a nimbus of intense white sparks, as it used its club hands to smash down the concertina wire and wade directly towards an arched tunnel that went through the Wall.

"I'm going to follow it," said Nick. "Pass the word not to shoot. If any other Scouts come up, tell them to stay back. This particular creature needs the blood of Charter Mages."

"Who should I say—"

Nick ignored him, heading west along the trench to the point where the creature had begun to force its path. There were no soldiers there, only the signs of a very rapid exodus, with equipment and weapons strewn across the trench floor.

Nick climbed out and started towards the Wall. It was night in the Old Kingdom, a darker night without the moon, but the star-shell light spread over the Wall, so he could see that it was snowing there, not a single snowflake coming south.

He lifted the daisy-chain wreath over his head and held it ready in his left hand, and he drew the dagger with his right. The flowers were crushed, and many had lost petals, but the chain was unbroken, thanks to the linen thread sewn into the stems. Llew and his nieces really had known their business.

Nick was halfway across the No Man's Land when the creature reached the Wall. But it did not enter the tunnel, hunkering down on its haunches for half a minute before it eased itself up and turned back. It was still surrounded by white sparks, and even thirty yards away Nick could smell the acrid stench of hot metal. He stopped too, and braced himself for a sudden, swift attack.

The creature slowly paced towards him. Nick lifted the wreath, and made ready to throw or swing it over the creature's head. But it didn't attack, or increase its pace. It walked up close and began to lower its head.

Nick didn't take his eyes off it for even a microsecond. As soon as he was sure of his aim, he tossed the wreath over the creature's head. The flowers settled on its shoulders, the yellow and red flowers taking on a bluish cast from the crackling sparks that jetted out from the creature's hide.

"Let us talk and make truce, as the day's eye bids me do," said a chill, sharp voice directly into Nick's head, or so it felt. His ears heard nothing but the wind flutes and the jangle of cans tied to the wire. "We have no quarrel, you and I."

"We do," said Nick. "You have slain many of my people. You would slay more."

The creature did not move, but Nick felt the mental equivalent of a snort of disbelief.

"These pale, insipid things? The blood of a great one moves in you, more than in any of the inheritors that I have drunk from before. Come, shed your transient flesh and travel with me, back to our own land, beyond this prison wall."

Nick didn't answer, for he was suddenly confused. Part of him felt that he could leave his body and go with this creature that had somehow become beautiful and alluring in his eyes. He felt he had the power to shuck his skin and become something else, something fierce and powerful and strange. He could fly over the Wall and go wherever he wanted, do whatever he wanted.

Against that yearning to be untrammelled and free was another set of sensations and desires. He did want to change, that was true, but he also wanted to continue to be himself. To be a man, to find out where he fitted in amongst people, specifically the people of the Old Kingdom, for he knew he could no longer be content in Ancelstierre. He wanted to see his friend Sam again, and he wanted to talk to Lirael…

"Come," said the creature again. "We must be away before any of Astarael's get come upon us. Share with me a little of your blood, so that I may cross this cursed wall without scathe."

"Astarael's get?" asked Nick. "The Abhorsens?"

"Call them what you will," said the creature. "One comes, but not soon. I feel it, through the bones of the earth beneath my feet. Let me drink, just a little."

"Just a little..." mused Nick. "Do you fear to drink more?"

"I fear," said the creature, bowing its head still lower. "Who would not fear the power of the Nine Bright Shiners, highest of the high?"

"What if I do not let you drink, and I do not choose to leave this flesh?"

"Your will is yours alone," said the creature. "I shall go back, and reap a harvest among those that bear the Charter, weak and prisoned remnant of my kin of long ago."

"Drink then," said Nick. He cut the bandage at his wrist and, wincing at the pain, sliced open the wound Dorrance had made. Blood welled up immediately.

The creature leaned forward and Nick turned his wrist so the blood fell into its open mouth, each drop sizzling as it met the thing's internal fires. A dozen drops fell, then Nick took his dagger again and cut more deeply. Blood gushed more freely, splashing over the creature's mouth.

"Enough!" said the voice in his mind. But Nick did not withdraw his hand, and the creature did not move. "Enough!"

Nick held his hand closer to the creature's mouth, sparks enveloping his fingers, to be met by golden flames, blue and gold twirling and wrestling, as if Charter Magic visibly sought dominance over Free Magic.

"Enough!" screamed the silent voice in Nick's head, driving out all other thoughts and senses, so that he became blind and dumb and couldn't feel anything, not even the rapid stammer of his own heartbeat. "Enough! Enough! Enough!"

It was too much for Nick's weakened body to bear. He faltered, his hand wavering. As the blood missed the creature's mouth, it staggered too, and fell to one side. Nick fell too, away from it, and the voice inside his head gave way to blessed silence.

His vision returned a few seconds later, and his hearing. He lay on his back, looking up at the sky. The moon was just about to set in the west, but it was like no moonset he had ever seen for the right corner of it was cut off diagonally by the Wall.

Nick stared at the bisected moon, and thought that he should get up and see if the creature was moving, if it was going to go and attack the soldiers in order to dilute his blood once again. He should bandage his wrist too, he knew, for he could feel the blood still dripping down his fingers.

But he couldn't get up. Whether it was blood-loss, or simply exhaustion from everything he'd been through, or the effects of the icy voice on his brain, he was as limp and helpless as a rag doll.

I'll gather my strength he thought, closing his eyes. *I'll get up in a minute. Just a minute...*

Something warm landed on his chest. Nick forced his eyes to open just enough to look out. The moon was much lower, now looking like a badly cut slice of pumpkin pie.

His chest got warmer again and, with the warmth, Nick felt just a tiny fraction stronger. He opened his eyes properly and managed to raise his head an inch off the ground.

A coiled spiral made up of hundreds of Charter marks was slowly boring its way into his chest, like some kind of celestial, star-wrought drill, all shining silver and gold. As each coil went in, Nick felt strength return to more far-flung parts of his body. His arms twitched and he raised them too, and saw a nice clean, Army-issue bandage around his wrist. Then he regained sensation in his legs and lifted them up, to see his carpet slippers had been replaced with more bandages.

"Can you hear me?" asked a soft voice, just out of sight. A woman's voice, familiar to Nick, though he couldn't place it for a second.

He turned his head. He was lying near the Wall, where he'd fallen. The creature was still lying there too, a few steps away. Between them, a young woman knelt over him. A young woman wearing an armoured coat of laminated plates, and over it a surcoat with the golden stars of the Clayr quartered with the silver keys of the Abhorsen.

"Yes," whispered Nick. He smiled and said, "Lirael."

Lirael didn't smile back. She brushed her black hair back from her face with a golden-gloved hand, and said,

"The spells are working strangely on you, but they are working. I'd best deal with the Hrule."

"The creature?"

Lirael nodded.

"Didn't I kill it? I thought my blood might poison it..."

"It has sated it," said Lirael. "And made it much more powerful, when it can digest it."

"You'd better kill it first, then."

"It can't be killed," said Lirael. But she picked up a very odd-looking spear, a simple shaft of wood that was topped with a fresh-picked thistle-head, and stepped over to the creature. "Nothing of stone or metal can pierce its flesh. But a thistle will return it to the earth, for a time."

She lifted the spear high above her head and drove it down with all her strength into the creature's chest. Surprisingly, the thistle didn't break on the hide that turned back bullets, but cut through as easily as a hand through water. The spear quivered there for a moment, then it burst, shaft and point together, like a mushroom spore. The dust fell on the creature, and where it fell, the flesh melted away, soaking into the ground. Within seconds there was nothing left, not even the glow of the violet eyes.

"How did you know to bring a thistle?" asked Nick, and then cursed himself for sounding so stupid. And for looking so pathetic. He raised his head again and tried to roll over, but Lirael quickly knelt and gently pushed him back down.

"I didn't. I arrived an hour ago, in answer to a rather confused message from the Magistrix at Wyverley. I expected merely to cross here, not to find one of the rarest of Free Magic creatures. And... and you. I bound your wounds and put some healing charms upon you, and then went to find a thistle."

"I'm glad it was you."

"It's lucky I read a lot of bestiaries when I was younger," said Lirael, who wouldn't look him in the eye. "I'm not sure even Sabriel would know about the peculiar nature of the Hrule. Well, I'd best be on my way. There are stretcher bearers waiting to come over to take you in. I think you'll be all right now. There's no lasting damage. Nothing from the Hrule, I mean. No new lasting effects, that is... I really do have to get going. Apparently there's some Dead thing or other further south, the message wasn't clear—"

"That was the creature," said Nick. "I sent a message to the Magistrix. I followed the creature all the way here from Dorrance Hall."

"Then I can go back to the Guards who escorted me here," said Lirael, but she made no move to go, just nervously parting her hair again with her golden-gloved hand. "They won't have started back for Barhedrin yet. That's where I left my Paperwing. I can fly by myself now. I mean, I'm still—"

"I don't want to go back to Ancelstierre," burst out Nick. He tried to sit up and this time succeeded, Lirael reaching out to help him and then letting go as if he were red hot. "I want to come to the Old Kingdom."

"But you didn't come before," said Lirael.."When we left and Sabriel said you should because of what... because of what had happened to you. I wondered, that is Sam thought later, perhaps you didn't want to, that is you needed to stay in Ancelstierre for some person, I mean reason—"

"No," said Nick. "There is nothing for me in Ancelstierre. I was afraid, that's all."

"Afraid?" asked Lirael. "Afraid of what?"

"I don't know," said Nick. He smiled again. "Can you give me a hand to get up? Oh, your hand! Sam really did make a new one for you!"

Lirael flexed her golden, Charter-spelled hand, opening and closing the fingers to show Nick that it was just as good as one of flesh and bone, before she gingerly offered both her hands to him.

"I've only had it for a week," she said shyly, looking down as Nick stood not very steadily beside her. "And I don't think it will work very far south of here. Sam really is a most useful nephew. Do you think you can walk?"

"If you help me," said Nick.

The OLD KINGDOM Series

Sabriel

One warrior to challenge the dead...

Lirael

Dark magic and destiny...

Abhorsen

The last hope for the living...

"Sabriel is a winner, a fantasy that reads like realism.
I congratulate Garth Nix." *Philip Pullman*

HarperCollins *Children's Books*

THE KEYS TO THE KINGDOM series

Seven days. Seven keys.
One mysterious book.
One strange house filled with secrets.

MISTER MONDAY

Arthur Penhaligon is not supposed to be a hero. He is
supposed to die. But then he meets sinister Mister
Monday and everything changes.

GRIM TUESDAY

When Arthur left the strange house that had almost
killed him on Monday, he didn't expect to be called
back there the very next day.

DROWNED WEDNESDAY

An invitation to lunch leads to a stormy voyage,
Nothing-laced gunpowder and pirates, landing
Arthur in very hot water indeed!

HarperCollins *Children's Books*